"Jake, we've had nothing more than polite conversation since I got back, and now, today, you kiss me like that?"

"I tried to talk to you, Lori. You weren't having it."

"You don't get a pass, Jake. The last time we had a conversation that lasted more than a minute was over the grave of our daughter."

"You wouldn't talk with me. Not about anything that mattered."

"Because I still have some pride left."

"So you're saying we need to talk first."

"First?" She met his gaze. "We have some things to work through. No matter how well we fit or how much I'm tempted, I know you, and you are not staying around after we sleep together."

"That's not true."

"No? Then let's tell your mother we're a couple."

"Is that what you want, Lori? To be a couple?"

"I don't know. But I sure know what I don't want. I don't want to be your dirty little secret. And I don't want you to hurt me again."

SURROGATE ESCAPE

JENNA KERNAN

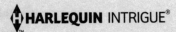
HARLEQUIN INTRIGUE®

For Jim, always.

ISBN-13: 978-1-335-52625-0

Surrogate Escape

Copyright © 2018 by Jeannette H. Monaco

Recycling programs
for this product may
not exist in your area.

Printed in U.S.A.

Jenna Kernan has penned over two dozen novels and has received two RITA® Award nominations. Jenna is every bit as adventurous as her heroines. Her hobbies include recreational gold prospecting, scuba diving and gem hunting. Jenna grew up in the Catskills and currently lives in the Hudson Valley in New York State with her husband. Follow Jenna on Twitter, @jennakernan, on Facebook or at jennakernan.com.

Books by Jenna Kernan

Harlequin Intrigue

Apache Protectors: Wolf Den

Surrogate Escape

Apache Protectors: Tribal Thunder

Turquoise Guardian
Eagle Warrior
Firewolf
The Warrior's Way

Apache Protectors

Shadow Wolf
Hunter Moon
Tribal Law
Native Born

Harlequin Historical

Gold Rush Groom
The Texas Ranger's Daughter
Wild West Christmas
A Family for the Rancher
Running Wolf

Harlequin Nocturne

Dream Stalker
Ghost Stalker
Soul Whisperer
Beauty's Beast
The Vampire's Wolf
The Shifter's Choice

Visit the Author Profile page at Harlequin.com.

CAST OF CHARACTERS

Jake Redhorse—The newest hire on the Turquoise Canyon tribal police force. Nothing matters to him more than his duty to protect his people.

Lori Mott—A nurse in the tribe's health clinic who was Jake's steady girlfriend in high school until a personal tragedy tore them apart. She wants only to heal the sick of their tribe and avoid the pain of seeing Jake.

Jack Bear Den—A Turquoise Guardian, the tribe's only detective and Jake's idol.

Ty Redhorse—Jake's troubled elder brother who has gang ties and a criminal past. He currently works as a mechanic detailing and repairing muscle cars. He and Jake rarely talk.

Kee Redhorse—The eldest of Jake's brothers and the family golden boy, he's a physician at the tribe's clinic.

Colt Redhorse—Jake's youngest brother, recently back from Iraq and suffering from PTSD.

Dr. Hector Hauser—The director of the tribe's health clinic and the mentor of Kee Redhorse.

Betty Mills—Longtime administrator of the tribe's health clinic.

Minnie Cobb—A gang member whose cooperation with tribal police sent her boyfriend to federal prison and earned her both a reduced sentence and the need to prove her loyalty to her gang.

Earle Glass—A gang member on Turquoise Canyon reservation and Minnie's new man.

Prologue

Why did the cramping continue even after she had delivered the baby? She waited out of sight, watching the road for the return of Officer Redhorse. It was cold, so she kept the wiggling girl inside her jacket against her skin, allowing her to suck. That was what babies liked, to be on their mother's skin. Only, she wasn't its mother. She'd seen enough of her brothers and sisters come home from the hospital to know that Apache babies did not have blond hair.

Finally, she spotted his squad car as he made the turn toward their street. Even in the predawn, she could make out the familiar dark, round image on the white panel of the door that she knew was the tribe's great seal. There was no time to reach his front step now. He was driving too fast, and she'd never make it back to cover before he spotted her. So she rushed from the tree line only as far as the back of his pickup, intending to wrap the baby in her own coat.

Climbing up onto the bumper was difficult with the use of only one hand. She glanced to the road. He was nearly here. She saw something in the truck bed, a garment, and she snatched it up, then bundled the little girl inside the fleece and laid her gently on the bed of the truck. If he didn't see the baby, she'd come back and get her, leave her on his doorstep, knock and run.

Why hadn't she thought of that before?

She draped one sleeve of the men's fleece jacket over the gate of the pickup bed and jumped down. The jolt of the landing made her hurt all over and she gave a sharp cry. She grabbed her middle with both hands as she hurried back to cover just as he made the turn into his driveway.

In the brush between the two houses, the girl pressed a hand to her mouth. Something was happening. Her body was clenching again as if she were still in labor. The cramp went all the way around her middle.

The door to Officer Redhorse's squad car opened and he stood, glancing around and then straight at her. She sank back. He'd seen her. Any second now he'd come over here and arrest her. She whimpered, choking the pain back far in her throat. Something issued from between her legs. She glanced down at the quivering purple thing. What was that? She poked at it and then stood. The umbilical cord that had still been attached to her body between her legs was fixed to the thing. It looked like her liver. She wondered if she would die without the organ. Clearly something inside had torn loose. But the bleeding was slowing.

She wasn't stupid. She knew how girls got pregnant, and she knew she'd never done anything like that with a boy. Yet she'd given birth to a baby. Could someone have done that to her while she was sleeping?

No, that just wasn't possible. Was it?

She looked back toward the driveway. Redhorse carried something in his arms as he disappeared into his home.

The girl staggered out once more and checked the truck. The baby was gone. She breathed a sigh and then turned toward home, her insides cramping, her legs trembling from the effort of bringing the baby into the world.

She crept away, holding her aching, sagging middle with both hands. No one was awake yet when she reached the bathroom to clean up. She was careful not to get blood on any of the towels. It was likely that her mother would not notice, or would blame the stain on her monthly cycle. Still, she could not take the chance.

With the amount of beer her mother had consumed, she knew that she wouldn't be up for hours. But her brothers and sisters would need to be fed. She'd stay long enough to do that, at least.

After removing her coat and shucking out of her shirt, she noticed the bloody imprint of the infant on her side. She swallowed the lump rising in her throat. She couldn't keep the baby. Not when someone wanted it badly enough to come to her house looking for her.

She had hidden the pregnancy and escaped the creepy pair who stalked her, even dropping out of school to avoid them. But they knew. Somehow, they knew about the pregnancy even before she did. Would they stop now?

Maybe if she showed up somewhere in something that proved she was no longer pregnant—but then they might wonder where it had gone. She finished washing and then headed back outside. The newborn was not her flesh. But she still needed to protect her. She would go see what Officer Redhorse was doing and make sure the baby was safe.

She'd stay long enough to do that, at least. Then she would run like Elsie. She had to, because they would come back. They always came back.

Chapter One

Officer Jake Redhorse turned into his driveway and caught movement in his periphery by the line of pine and sticker bushes to his left. The fatigue must be affecting his vision, because when he turned toward his neighbor's yard, there was nothing there.

Jake put his police unit into Park in the usual place, behind his silver F-150 pickup. That was when he noticed the red cloth hanging out of the back of his truck bed. That had not been there when he'd pulled in from his last shift sometime Thursday night, which was two days ago. Shifts had been unpredictable since the dam breech.

He stared at the red fleece. Someone had been messing with his truck.

"They better not have busted into my tools," he muttered and left his police unit, using his fob to lock the car. He needed to remove the shotgun and his personal gear from the trunk and take them inside, but first he had to see what the vandals had done to his vehicle.

Since the collapse of the Skeleton Cliff Dam just

this week, there was an uptick in petty crime, including a number of break-ins of the houses left behind in the ongoing relocation effort, and apparently being a cop did not exempt him from vandalism.

His small police force of seven struggled to keep order and so, five days after the explosion, his tribal council voted to accept the help of the National Guard to keep order in the tribal seat in Piñon Forks. The council also agreed to allow FEMA to provide temporary housing for the low-lying communities along the river. And now the Army Corps of Engineers was helping plan a more stable temporary dam to support the pile of rubble that had stopped the water and saved his people. But the outsiders were not allowed to venture past the river town. So his small police force was stretched over the two remaining communities of Turquoise Ridge and Koun'nde, on the Turquoise Canyon Apache Reservation, where he lived. Even with outsider help, his shifts were still way too long.

"Ah, not my drill," he said, hope butting up against apprehension.

When Jake left his vehicle and approached the tailgate of his truck, he had the distinct feeling of being watched. A sweeping search of his surroundings showed no one. But the hairs on his neck remained raised like the scruff of a barking dog. He could still see his breath in the cool mountain air. Late September was like that here. Cold nights. Warm, dry days.

"Hello?" he called and received no answer but the autumn wind. Jake turned his collar up against the chill.

He glanced over the tailgate into the truck bed, now recognizing the red cloth. It was a polar-fleece jacket his mother had given him. He disliked red for several reasons—for one, it reminded him of a target, which, as a police officer, he already was, and for another, it reminded him of the iconic red trade cloth his people, the Tonto Apache, had once tied around their foreheads to keep the Anglos from shooting them by accident during the Apache Wars. His tribe had fought with the US Army in that one. Finally, the cloth reminded him of Lori Mott, as it was her favorite color.

The jacket was wet. He glanced down at the fabric, which was wrapped around something. At first he thought it was a child's doll. Then the doll moved.

Jake jumped back, hand going automatically to his service weapon, a .45 caliber, as his brain tried to make sense of what he had seen. He had his flashlight out in a moment and shone it on the bundle.

The tiny forehead wrinkled. It was a baby, ghastly pale, its skin translucent with something that looked like a sheet of white tissue hanging from it. The baby's mouth opened, and a thready sound emerged.

Jake jumped back again. Someone had left a baby in the bed of his truck. A baby!

He lifted his radio from his hip and called for an ambulance. The reply came from the volunteer fire station back in Piñon Forks, who answered calls after-hours. Unfortunately, the tribe's one ambulance was currently out on a run all the way up in Turquoise Ridge, so they told him to call the urgent-care clinic.

At twenty-one, Jake was the tribe's most recent hire, and his utility belt was so new that the leather squeaked when he replaced the radio to the holster. He drew out his mobile phone and called his brother Kee. The eldest of the family, Kee had been recently certified in internal medicine—the first board-certified physician in many years. The phone rang five times and then flipped to voice mail. Jake left a message before disconnecting. There was always the chance that the clinic might still be open. If any of the women of his tribe had given birth last night, the maternity ward and nursery would be staffed. If not, they wouldn't open until nine o'clock in the morning. Jake's emotions warred with one another. He needed help. But there was a possibility that his help might be Lori Mott.

She'd come back last September and had done a very effective job of letting him know that bygones would not be bygones. She seemed mad at him, though he didn't know why. Their one encounter had been consensual, though they had both been underage at the time. The resulting unplanned pregnancy was certainly both of their faults. He'd done the responsible thing. Everyone said so.

Jake blew out a breath and dialed the number.

Not her. Not her. Not her. He chanted the words in his head like a prayer, hoping to will Lori from answering his call.

Lori worked at the clinic most days and nights as needed, along with Nina Kenton, Verna Dia and Burl Tsosie. Everyone was working long hours since the dam collapse. But even after all this time, speaking to her roiled up his emotions and made his stomach flip. The quicksilver attraction to Lori was still there, at least for him, but it was tempered by her obvious dislike of him. He didn't understand it. Everybody liked him—everyone but Lori.

His heart rate increased as he clutched the mobile phone, scowling that his body reacted to just the possibility of speaking to her. How many times did a man have to stick his finger into a light socket before he figured out what would happen next?

"Jake?"

Lori Mott's familiar voice came through. His number would have displayed his name, giving her fair warning, yet he was rattled at the control in her voice. His body flashed hot and cold, the desire that lived just beneath his skin and the regret that clung to him like pine pitch.

His heart beat faster.

The surprise was gone from her voice, and her tone now held an edge of warning. "Jake."

"Hi, Lori." He felt as if his mouth were full of pebbles, and he couldn't quite speak past them. Instead, something like a gurgle emerged from his throat. He stared at the newborn lying in his truck bed and plunged on. "I found a baby, and the ambulance is out at Turquoise Ridge."

"Possible heart attack," she said. "They're going to Darabee."

She tied his stomach in knots quicker than a Boy Scout going for a merit badge. He could picture her, standing in those scrubs she always wore, with her long hair scraped back in a high ponytail for work. Often she wore no makeup. Not that she needed any.

"Did you say you found a baby?" she asked.

"Yes."

"Where? When?" Her voice took on a breathy air that made his skin tingle.

"Just now. Someone left it in the bed of my pickup."

"Outside?" Her voice rang with alarm. "Is it breathing?"

"Crying."

"Is it cold?"

"I haven't touched it."

"Jake. For goodness' sake, pick it up."

He closed his eyes, recalling the last infant he had held, cold as marble and gray as a tombstone. He started sweating.

"I don't know how to pick up a baby," he said.

"I'm on my way. I'll bring my kit. Is it a newborn?"

"It's really small. Like the size of a doll. And wet."

"Wet?" She told him how to pick it up. He lifted the infant and the red fleece all together, supporting the baby's tiny head.

"It's warm," he said, juggling the phone as he cradled the newborn. "It's got blood on it and some skin or something."

"Take it inside. Wrap it up in something dry and wait for me. Did you call Child Protective Services?"

At her question, he recalled that his training included instructions to call the state agency, and that he had the number saved in his contacts on his phone.

"Not yet."

"I'll do it." The phone went dead.

Jake held the still bundle and the phone. He glanced around one last time.

"Hello?"

The morning chill seeped under his collar as he stood holding the infant before him like a live grenade. He thought he might be sick as past and present collided in his mind. Lori was coming. Sweet Lord, Lori was coming. He squeezed his eyes closed. The sound of movement made them flash open, and he turned toward the rustling.

"Is anyone there?"

Nothing moved but the little baby pressed against his chest.

LORI DROVE TOWARD Koun'nde in the rising light before dawn. Burl had arrived quickly to relieve her, and so she was only a few minutes away from having to face Jake Redhorse. Since her return, she had mostly avoided him. It was infuriating how he could still make her tremble with just a smile. One thing was certain. She was not falling for his charm twice.

As she approached his home, the anxiety and determination rolled inside her like a familiar tide. If she had not been good enough for him then, she was now. Only, now she didn't want him, the jerk.

She'd learned what he really thought of her after the baby had come. Not from him, of course. Oh, no. Mr. Wonderful would never insult a woman. He'd left that to everyone else.

Damn him.

Her face heated at the shame of it, still, always.

She pulled into the drive, wondering if she had the courage to make the walk to his front step. As it turned out, she didn't have to. Jake hurled himself out the front door without his familiar white Stetson or uniform jacket and charged her driver's side like a bull elk.

"Hurry," he said.

Lori grabbed her tote and medical bag and followed as Jake reversed course and dashed back into his home. Lori ran, too, her medical bag thumping against her thigh as she cleared the door. Once inside, she heard the angry squall of a newborn.

Jake stopped in the living room before a dirty red polar fleece, which sat beside a couch cushion on his carpet. On the wide cushion was a baby wrapped in a familiar fuzzy green knit blanket, its tiny face scrunched and its mouth open wide as it howled. Lori's stride faltered. She knew that blanket because she had knit it herself from soft, mint-colored yarn. She glanced at Jake. Why had he kept it?

Jake pointed at the baby. "It's turning purple."

Chapter Two

Lori scooped up the infant and cradled the tiny newborn against her chest. The sharp stab of grief pierced her heart. She'd held dozens of newborns since that day, but none had been wrapped in her blanket and Jake had not been standing at her side. It was all too familiar. She tried to hide the tears, but with both hands on her charge she could not wipe them away.

Jake stepped up beside her and rested a once-familiar hand on her shoulder. His touch stirred memories of pleasure and shame, and her chin dropped as she nestled her cheek against the fuzzy head that rooted against her neck.

She turned and allowed herself to really look at Jake. Oh, she had seen him since her return, often in fact, but she'd refused to let herself look, refused to allow the emotional gate to swing open. But the baby and the blanket had tripped some switch and she wanted to see him again, if only to remember why she had once loved him. Permission granted to herself, she braced for the pain. His brow had grown more prominent, and his broad forehead was made wider because his hair was tugged back in a single pony at his neck, which was dressed with blue cloth. He always wore blue now.

No, not always, she remembered. Once, he'd worn his hair wrapped in red cloth. Jake's ears showed at each side of his head and she noticed they seemed tucked back, as if he needed to hear something behind him. He wore a silver stud in each ear. Police regulations required that he wore nothing dangling, but she preferred the long silver feathers she'd given him. Did he ever wear them?

His jaw was more prominent now, having grown sharp and strong. The taut skin of his cheeks seemed darker than the rest of his face due to a day's growth of stubble. She traced the blade of a nose with her gaze, ending at his mouth, and watched his nostrils flare and his lips part. Their eyes met and she went still, seeing the familiar warm amber brown of his eyes. He still made her insides quake and her heart pound. Memories swirled as he took a step forward. He rested his hands on her shoulders and angled his jaw.

Oh, no. He's going to kiss me.

Instead of revulsion, her body furnished blazing desire. She told herself to step back but found herself stepping forward. The newborn in her arms gave a bleat like a baby lamb, bringing her back to her senses. Had she been about to stroke that familiar face?

She stiffened. Damned if she'd give him the chance to hurt her again. She was through with men who treated her like she wasn't good enough. There were men out there who judged you by yourself instead of by your family. Jake Redhorse was simply not one of them.

"I'm sorry, Lori."

She narrowed her eyes at him and made a disbelieving sound in her throat. Was he sorry that she'd come, sorry that he'd nearly kissed her or sorry that anyone else in the world was not here to help him?

His mother would have been an option—his mother, who had called her an apple, red on the outside and white on the inside, because her father had been white. Then she'd called her siblings pieces in a fruit basket. Lori was well aware that none of her siblings shared the same father, because no one ever let her forget it.

His mother had disliked her right from the start, but after May Redhorse learned about Lori's condition and that Jake planned to marry her, her dislike solidified to distain. Mrs. Redhorse was a good Christian and a bad person.

Finally, belatedly, Lori stepped back. Jake's eyes still had that piercing look of desire. She drew a breath as she prepared to throw cold water on him.

"You could have called your mom," she said. Bringing up his mother was a sure way to douse the flame that had sprung from cold ashes between them.

His mouth twisted. "She can't get around very well right now."

Lori recalled the diabetes and the toe amputation— more than one. His mother had always been a big woman, and the disease had only made her less mobile. Some of her anger leaked away.

"Yes, of course."

"What's wrong with it?" asked Jake, pointing to the fussing infant.

"Hungry, maybe. Let's have a look."

Lori found Jake's kitchen and laid the baby on his dinette. Then she peeled back the blanket and stroked the knit edge.

"You kept it," she said.

"Yeah."

"Why?"

"Just reminds me of her."

Lori didn't need a reminder. She carried the memories in her heart like a spike. The baby girl she'd lost. Jake's baby. At the time she thought the miscarriage was her fault, that she must have done something wrong. She knew better now.

The baby before them had ceased fussing and stared up at them with wide blue eyes. The infant was pink and white, with skin so translucent you could see the tiny veins that threaded across her chest and forehead. She was clearly a newborn, still streaked with her mother's blood.

Lori shrugged out of her coat and Jake stepped forward to take it. Always the gentleman, she thought. Perfect as Captain Freakin' America. Captain of the soccer team, basketball team and track team. Fast, smart and somehow once interested in her. The world made no sense.

"What's that white stuff?" he asked, peering over her shoulder, his breath warm and sweet on her neck.

"That's the caul. It's the tissue sack that surrounds the baby in the womb. I hear that some Anglos believe that wearing the caul is lucky."

"What Anglos?"

"The Irish, I think. Maybe Scottish. I can't recall. My granddad was a Scot." Why did she feel the need to remind him her father had not been Apache?

JAKE GLANCED AT HER, letting the desire build again. He knew her grandfather had been a Scot. He even remembered her father. He'd been a redhead who worked for the oil and gas company in Darabee for a while. He was the reason that Lori's hair took on a red gleam in the sunlight. She'd taken a lot of teasing over that in grade school. She even had a light dusting of freckles over her nose. Or she had as a child, anyway. It made her different. Jake thought those differences made her more beautiful, but he'd been one of the worst in middle school. Anything to get her attention, even if it was only to see her flush and storm off.

Lori had changed over the five years of separation, and at age twenty-one, she had grown into a woman's body. Her skin was a healthy golden brown and her mouth was still full but tipped down at the corners. Above the delicate nose, her dark brows arched regally over the deep brown eyes. The sadness he saw there was new. Today she wore her long, thick hair coiled in a knot at the base of her skull, practical like her uniform. And the hairstyle disguised the soft natural wave in her hair. Lori worked with children and babies, so her top was always alive with something bright and cheerful. Today it was teddy bears all tumbling down her chest with blocks. The bottoms matched, picking up the purples of the top and hugging her hips. The shoes were slip-on clogs with rubber soles. White, of course.

But beneath the trim medical nurses' scrubs, he knew her body. Or he'd known the body of her youth. His fingers itched to explore the changes, the new fullness of her breasts and the tempting flare of her hips. They were children no longer, so before he went down this road again, he needed to think first. He hadn't thought the last time.

Actions had consequences. He knew that well enough by now.

She had been a pretty girl but had become a classic beauty of a woman. When she danced at powwows, she drew the photographers like a blossom drew bees. The camera loved her, and he had a copy of a magazine where she'd been chosen as a cover model back in their senior year. Dressed in her regalia, she had a poise and intelligence that shone past the bright beads around her neck and white paint that ran down her lip to her chin. The cover that should have been a coup turned into another source for teasing as the lighting highlighted that her brown eyes were more cinnamon and revealed red highlights in her hair. Where was that magazine? His eyes popped open and he glanced about his living space, hoping she wouldn't spot it before he could tuck it away.

Lori continued on, "My grandmother, my dad's mother, told me once to look out for a baby with a caul. It means the baby is special."

"All babies are special," he said, thinking of one in particular.

LORI GLANCED AT the newborn, a little girl, checking her toes and fingers and finding her perfectly formed, if somewhat small.

"Do you have a kitchen scale?"

"A what?"

She smiled. "No way to check her weight, then. Grab my medical kit."

Jake darted away as Lori examined the umbilical cord. Someone had tied it with a strip of green bark over a foot from the baby and then sliced the cord cleanly through. It was not the sort of cut a midwife would make, and it was not the sort of twine you would find in a home. More like the materials someone who had given birth outdoors would use.

Her mind leaped immediately to a teenage mother. Lori checked the baby and found nothing to indicate where the child had been born, but by the look of her, she was white.

"Here it is." Jake set the kit down on the chair with a thump.

"Hold on to her so she doesn't fall," said Lori.

"Hold on how?"

Lori wrapped the baby again and then took his big, familiar hand and placed it on the baby's chest.

"Easy. Don't press."

Then she retrieved a diaper from a side pocket. When she returned, it was to find him using a piece of gauze to wipe the blood from the infant's face.

"We'll do that at the clinic," she said.

"It's a blood sample," he said. "Mother's blood, right?"

She stilled. What she had seen as a childcare issue he saw as a crime scene.

"It's probably some scared kid," she said.

"It's a felony. There are places to bring a baby. Safe places. She left it outside in my truck."

She looked down at the tiny infant. Someone had given birth and then dumped her on a windy, cold September morning. She had treated babies abandoned by mothers before. They did not all survive. This little one was very lucky.

"Fortunate," she said.

He met her gaze.

"To be alive," she qualified.

Jake nodded. "I think she was still out there, watching me."

"The mother?"

He nodded.

"That's likely. She would have been close. Any idea who?"

"I need to take a look around the house."

She nodded. "Go on, then."

Jake tucked the gauze into one of the evidence

baggies he had on his person and then slipped it into one of the many pockets of his tribal police uniform.

"Done with your evidence collection?" she asked.

He nodded. "For now."

"Then I'll get the little one fed and ready to transport while you have your look around."

"Did you call Protective Services?" he asked.

"Betty called while I got my kit." Betty Mills was her boss and the administrator of the Tribal Health Clinic. "She said they have to contact whoever is on call in our area. It could be a while."

"Do you have a car seat for a newborn?" he asked, the unease settling in his chest.

Lori readied the diaper. "Yes. In my trunk. I'll bring her to the clinic for a checkup. Unclaimed babies always come to the clinic now. Do you think the mother could still be out there?"

"I'll know soon." He zipped his police jacket and replaced the white, wide-brimmed Stetson to his head. Then he cast her a long look that made her stomach quiver. She pressed her lips together, bracing against her physical reaction. *Fool me once*, she thought. "Thanks for coming, Lori."

"You want me to wait?" she asked.

"Yeah."

She nodded and watched him go. Jake Redhorse was her poison, but she was not going to be the tribe's source of gossip again. She couldn't go back and fix what was broken between them. Only he could do that, and it would mean admitting he had protected his reputation at the expense of hers. Left her out in the storm that never reached him. His luck, his reputation, his honor and his willingness to do what was right had all played in his favor. While her family legacy had cast her in the worst light. The natural scapegoat for daring to taint the reputation of the tribe's golden boy.

So, you're saying it's mine? That was what he'd actually said to her. He wasn't the first to suspect she'd pulled a fast one. How could they be so willing to think so little of her? After the gossip flew, she became the target of disdain. Her appearance in the classroom drew long silences, followed by snickering behind raised hands. Meanwhile, everyone felt sorry for Jake. Forgave him instantly. Who could blame him? He'd been tricked. Swindled. Seduced.

During junior year, Jake was still playing soccer and planned to play basketball but was already planning to get a part-time job moving cattle when the baby came.

When she mentioned her intention to work at the Darabee hospital as a health care aide, he'd scoffed.

"Finish high school, Lori," he'd said. "So you don't end up like your mom."

So he'd planned to drop out and have her stay in school. More fuel to make him the hero and her the parasite.

She had glared at him. "You could still go to college."

"No. I'll be here for my child."

Yes. Of course he would. But he had never had to. Instead, he had accepted condolences first for the unplanned pregnancy and later for his loss. His loss. Never *their* loss. She clamped her teeth together as the fury spiked. Instead, he had finished high school and gone to college and she had gone. too. Become a nurse. Shown them all. Only, no one had really noticed or cared.

Yet one look at the wiggling, smiling baby and her temper ebbed. As she looked down into her eyes, she felt a tug in her belly and breasts.

She knew this feeling, had felt it once before, even though her baby had already left.

Uh-oh, she thought. *Pair bonding*, her mind supplied, as if reviewing for one of her tests in school. That magic thing that made a baby uniquely yours.

"Don't do this, Lori," she warned herself. But it was already too late.

JAKE WALKED AROUND the truck. The wind had picked up so much that it whistled through the trees. Cold sunlight poured in golden bands through the breaks in the tall pines to the east. Behind the truck, he found a bloody palm print on his tailgate and pine needles beside the hitch. It looked as if someone had stepped on the bumper and then hoisted up to place the baby in the bed of the truck. She was small, then.

Had she arranged the red cloth so that he would notice it immediately against the silver of the F-150's body?

He could see no blood on the ground and no tracks on the earth on either side of the driveway. He cast his gaze about, looking for a place where she could have watched his arrival and still have been shielded from discovery. Then he walked to the most logical spot. There in the eastern row of piñon pine, at the base of one of the large trunks, was a spot where the needles had been disturbed. He squatted and saw that some-one had been here, waiting, evidenced by the sweep of a foot back and forth, creating two little mounds of needles and a swath of clean dark earth in between. He could not stand in the spot without hitting his head on the branches, but if he crouched down, he had a perfect view of the road and his driveway and the back of his pickup.

So she'd waited here, holding the infant, and then seeing his police cruiser make the turn onto his road... He checked the distance and imagined the timing. She, this brand-new mother, must have hur-ried out to the drive. He could see it now, the soft in-dentation of her foot. No boots. A sneaker, maybe. Small with little tread. She would have had to be quick, her hands likely still covered with the blood of the birth. Who had helped her bring the baby? He could find no evidence of a second person.

Did the father know she had left his child? The ache in his heart hardened in his belly.

He walked the perimeter of his property. Farther back, between his home and the pasture beyond, was something purple and bloody. He slowed his steps, approaching carefully. It was a placenta; he knew that from calving. The flies had found it already. He lifted his radio and called it in.

Carol Dorset, their dispatcher, was in the office

now and picked up on the first ring. Carol had been on dispatch back before Jake could even remember and had been the one to answer the phone the night Jake had to call 911 on his daddy.

"Chief's not here yet."

He glanced at his watch and noted it was 9:05 a.m. The shifts started at 7:00 a.m. and were staggered throughout the day. Since the explosion, they rotated covering nights. They were expecting two new hires, one patrol and one detective, but they had not started yet.

"Should I call the chief at home?" asked Jake. Since he hadn't been on the job very long, he wasn't sure what to do.

"I wouldn't," said Carol.

"What about Detective Bear Den?" he asked.

"He just left about thirty minutes ago. You can call him. I won't."

Tribal Police Detective Jack Bear Den had been out with him last night on the fatality involving a car and a tree. An outsider leaving their casino too late and too drunk. Jake had been first on scene and then Bear Den. Arizona Highway Patrol was next, and then the meat wagon.

He signed off the radio and replaced it to his side, then he retrieved his phone and hesitated, debating whether to call. If he waited, Bear Den might be asleep. He might even be already.

The dam breach and the aftermath was more than they could handle, which was why Bear Den had asked Jake to interview the family of the latest runaway, Maggie Kesselman. She'd be gone a week tomorrow. Girls had been disappearing since last November. There were always runaways among their tribe, but Bear Den had a hunch these girls had not taken off for Phoenix or Vegas. He said that there was something different happening, and he'd had Jake do some initial legwork when he'd been tied up with the dam breech.

Jake considered calling Ty. His older brother had a very good tracking dog who could find this new mother. He stared down at his phone.

He had not spoken to Ty in a long time. Too long. But since Jake had become a tribal police officer seven months ago, Ty was even more distant. Jake wondered what Ty would think if he asked him to chase down a criminal. He'd laugh, if he decided to pick up his phone.

Ty had gotten the worst of it from their dad, no doubt. He just couldn't shut his mouth or back down. Jake admired that, even though it brought Ty trouble more often than not.

Jake now felt a cold that had nothing to do with the wind. The blood trail from the placenta vanished in the tall grass. It occurred to him that if he'd walked to his back window with the baby, he might have seen the infant's mother escaping through the pasture behind his place. But he hadn't.

Had she paused here? Had she crept up to his window to peer inside?

Jake lifted his cell phone and called Detective Bear

Den. This was a crime scene and he didn't want to screw things up.

Bear Den picked up on the second ring, his voice gravelly. Jake's stomach dropped because he was certain Bear Den had just gotten to sleep. Jake explained the situation. Bear Den gave him instructions and told him he'd be there soon. The line went dead. Jake returned his phone to his pocket and finished circling the property, finding no further evidence.

The wind pushed at him, and he turned back to the house and the infant—and Lori. She seemed mad at him. But she had no reason to be. He'd asked her to marry him, hadn't he? He'd been willing to go through with it, too.

Ironic, he thought. An unexpected pregnancy had torn them apart and now, it seemed, had brought her back to him again. Well, he wasn't sixteen this time. Back then, he'd actually thought he loved Lori. But then they lost the baby and she acted as if he'd done something wrong, instead of everything right. He didn't understand her. It was as if she'd gone crazy. Even as he saw his dreams collapsing. Even knowing that he'd never become a police officer. He'd been willing to drop out of high school, give up college and marry her. He would have done it, against his mother's wishes, against his brother Ty's advice, he would have given his baby his name. And after they told him she had lost the baby, he hadn't left her. He'd gone to see her, to comfort her, and when they finally let him in to see Lori, she'd yelled at him.

He remembered exactly what she had said. *The only mistake I made was saying yes.*

Then she'd sent him off. Him!

Ty had called from boot camp just before Lori delivered and told him that Lori's older sisters Amelia and Jocelyn had each tried the same thing on Kee the minute he'd been accepted to college. Jocelyn had been only thirteen at the time. Amelia had moved on to Kurt Bear Den but ended up snagging Kent Haskie. Kent had married Amelia senior year and then gone to trade school to learn to fix air and cooling systems. They were still married and had four kids. Jocelyn had married Doug Hoke after their child was born in Jocelyn's junior year. Ty had told him Doug didn't know if he was the father, said it was hard to tell without a test and Jocelyn had been a popular girl. Kee had said Lori had targeted the best, just like a hunter assessing a herd of elk. That comment still chafed.

He didn't like being used, and he was not going to let that happen ever again. Still, he had never blamed Lori. He knew he'd made a mistake and had accepted responsibility. What more did she want?

Everyone thought he'd broken it off. Oh, no. She had. Firmly and irrevocably. He didn't understand it or her. And he didn't trust her. His confusion had kept him at a distance.

He didn't date women he didn't trust, and he did not trust Lori.

So why had he almost kissed her?

Chapter Three

"Any idea who left the baby?" asked Detective Bear Den.

The questions came more quickly when his boss, Wallace Tinnin, had arrived in a walking cast and come to a halt in Jake's driveway, wincing. The chief of tribal police had broken his ankle in the dam explosion and flat-out refused to use crutches. Judging from his sour expression and the circles under his eyes, he needed them—along with about ten hours of sleep.

This man had been a police officer for as long as Jake could remember and had come to his childhood home more than once. On one memorable visit, Tinnin had arrested both Jake's father and Ty in the same day.

Jake answered all the questions and Bear Den went off to examine the crime scene, otherwise known as Jake's home.

"You did a good job today, son," said Tinnin.

The praise was like a balm to his spirit and made his throat tighten. Tinnin had been the father figure Jake had chosen, a kind, decent man with an even, predictable temper. He was sparing with praise, which made it all the more precious when it was doled out.

"Thanks."

"You two getting back together?"

Tinnin knew all about them, of course. The entire tribe did. For a time there, he and Lori were the favorite topic of gossip, a cautionary tale and then a sad story that made folks shake their heads.

Isn't that a shame about Jake Redhorse? I'm not surprised about the Mott girl, but Redhorse...you'd think he'd know better.

He unlocked his jaw to speak. "No, sir. I just called her because both the ambulance and my brother Kee were unavailable."

"I see. Last choice, huh? Funny, though. You two losing a baby girl and then you two finding one, what, three years later?"

"Five." March sixteenth, just two days after his own birthday. And the wedding was exchanged for a funeral. The white dress stored and the black dress purchased. Jake's mother had been relieved that he would not have to marry "that girl." He'd worn his first suit, his wedding suit, to his daughter's funeral. His upper and lower teeth collided again, and he ground them side to side.

Jake looked away. He'd been a good kid and made his mother proud, mostly. And he'd always tried to give her something, anything to bring her joy. His dad had been in prison, his oldest brother in medical school, and Ty was shipping out on his first tour. He'd been the man of the house at sixteen, and he'd made a mistake with Lori.

"Have you seen the baby yet?" asked Jake.

Tinnin's thick brows lifted, and he gave a shake of his head. His boss was thin to the point of being gaunt. Gray streaked his collar-length hair in a way that made it look as if he'd accidentally leaned into a freshly painted wall, the white clinging to just the top layer of his scalp. The bags and circles under his eyes were perpetual. His jeans and denim coat made him look like a cowboy, unless you noted the shield clipped to his belt and the bulge where he wore his .45 caliber pistol.

"Why would I need to see her?"

"She has blue eyes," said Jake.

"All babies have blue eyes. No pigment yet."

"And blond hair."

Tinnin shifted, taking the pressure off his injured foot. "You think that baby is white?"

"Seemed so. I was there when Mom brought Abbie home, and I've been on a call for a woman delivering."

"Genevieve Ruiz," he said.

Jake nodded. "I've seen newborn Apache babies. This one is different."

"Might go see for myself."

"I'll come with you."

They headed to town in separate vehicles. Tinnin followed Jake to the tribe's urgent-care facility. Tinnin parked in a handicapped spot, and Jake walked slowly beside him through the emergency intake area. They passed Verna Dia heading for her car. She cast them a wave and tossed her bag into her passenger seat.

Inside the urgent-care area, they were greeted and waved on by another nurse, Nina Kenton. There was staff on duty now and patients already waiting. The clinic wasn't open overnight, though they did have a few rooms if they needed them, but that meant one of the staff had to work overtime, which cost money. The clinic was only six years old, furnished by casino profits, and it ran a deficit every year.

They waved to familiar faces as they headed to the baby wing, as Jake called it. This was a unique section of the facility, the women's health clinic, and included birthing rooms, exam rooms and a nursery. They found Lori with the chief physician, Dr. Hector Hauser, in the nursery, both wearing surgical masks over their faces. The bassinets were lined up but mostly empty. Jake spotted only two tiny sleeping faces.

This, then, was why Lori had been at work so early. She had become the favored delivery nurse because, according to their dispatcher, Lori was gaining clinical experience in preparation for taking the certification exam to become a neonatal nurse. She spent her life trying to bring healthy babies into the world, and Jake had to wonder at that. He also wondered why she had not married. Of the Mott sisters, only Lori and Dominique were single, and Dominique was still in high school. The Mott girls had a family history of marrying young and filling the tribe's rosters with new members.

Tinnin paused at the locked door to the nursery.

They could go no farther without access. This area remained locked to keep unauthorized people from doing something stupid, like snatching a baby, but they could see in through the viewing window.

Dr. Hauser had the tiny girl on a digital scale as she kicked and fussed, with Lori standing watch. Hauser's jowly face made him look both sad and serious. Unlike many in their tribe, Hauser kept fit and trim, but the lines at his eyes and the flesh at his neck told that he was well past his middle years.

The doctor leaned in, speaking to Lori, who recorded something—the weight, Jake assumed—in the chart neatly held to the metal clipboard.

Lori then set aside the chart and expertly lifted the tiny pink girl and bundled her in a soft-looking flannel wrap. She placed the girl on her shoulder and did a little bounce to comfort the infant. She seemed completely relaxed with a baby on her shoulder. Jake found himself smiling. It was at that moment she turned and noticed him there. Their gazes met, and she smiled back. He knew this by the crinkling of her eyes at the corners. She turned the newborn so he could see the tiny face, as if he were the nervous father coming to see his baby girl. Lori nodded at the baby and then glanced back to him. *Look what we did*, she seemed to say. *We saved this little one.*

He nodded, his smile broadening as a familiar warmth welled inside him. This was how she had once looked at him, and he missed it.

The warm welcome in Lori's eyes as she continued the rhythmic bounce made her look so different from how he usually saw her. They'd begun a routine of her spotting him when he had business at the clinic and him pretending not to see her, his eyes shifting away as he searched for an escape route. The only time he allowed himself to look at her was when she didn't know he was there. Until today. Now he saw her and she saw him. Something inside his chest tightened.

Tinnin made a sound in his throat. "That baby is white."

"I think so," said Jake.

"All white, I mean."

"Agreed."

"So, if the papa wasn't Apache, why would a white girl come up here to have a baby?"

Lori set the sleeping baby into the bassinet and then let Chief Tinnin and Jake Redhorse into the delivery room. Hauser lowered his mask to offer a greeting as he stepped past them. Then he headed down the corridor toward the urgent-care area and the patients already waiting. Lori offered her two visitors both a mask. Tinnin's limp was growing worse by the minute.

"How is she?" asked Tinnin, holding the mask to his face.

"She's perfect. A little small but otherwise healthy." She glanced at Jake, keeping her distance. The joy had fled, and now her steady gaze held a familiar caution.

Her attention flicked back to the chief.

"We need a blood type," said Tinnin.

"We do that routinely. I'll be sure you get a copy of the results."

"What about the baby?" Jake interjected.

"I'll be here until Burl arrives."

Burl Tsosie was one of the four nurses here, along with Lori, Nina and Verna.

"Any word from Protective Services?" asked Tinnin.

"Not yet, but they usually make us the temporary guardians. That gives them time to secure placement, if the mother isn't found."

"She's not getting that baby even if she is found." Jake's outrage crept into his voice. "Because I'm placing her under arrest."

Lori's eyes rolled up, and the breath she let out was audible.

He glanced at the baby, sleeping peacefully, her tiny eyelashes fanning her pink cheeks. She'd be placed and adopted, he realized. Why did that eventuality make his chest ache? He met Lori's gaze and saw she also looked troubled. They'd found her, and somehow that gave him a personal stake in what happened to this baby girl.

"When?" said Tinnin, referring to the arrival of a Protective Services representative.

"I'm not sure," said Lori. "They have an office in Globe and one in Flagstaff. Depends on what other business they have."

"I'll stay," said Jake.

Lori's brow wrinkled. "It might not even be today."

Jake set his jaw but said nothing.

Tinnin cast him an odd look.

"It's a lock-in area," Lori said to Jake, offering her

upturned hands with her explanation. "No one but the parents get near one of our babies."

"I'm still staying."

It was clear from the placement of one hand on her hip that Lori did not appreciate his intrusion into her territory.

Jake and Lori squared off.

Tinnin turned to hobble toward the door, pausing to look back at Jake. "Suit yourself, Redhorse. You're off duty. But try to get a few hours sleep."

The door closed behind him, and the chief wobbled past the viewing window and out of sight.

Lori returned her attention to Jake.

"Mask," she said, pointing to the mask he now held at his side.

He tied the top string around his head, then looked down at the newborn he'd found in his truck. She was very pale, but beautiful. He'd never thought babies were beautiful before. His chest ached again, and he itched to hold her. He reached out with one finger to stroke the infant's cheek.

"Don't touch the babies. You're not clean." Her crisp tone let him know that this was very definitely her dominion, and she did not appreciate him inserting himself here.

He wished he could keep the baby. Jake frowned. Of all the stupid ideas in his life, that fleeting thought was second only to the idea that he could control himself in the bed of his new pickup with Lori Mott back on that long-ago summer night when they were both sixteen. He never had been able to control himself around Lori.

Still couldn't. She riled him up. It was one of her special talents—making him crazy for her without seeming to do anything at all. He'd been young and dumb.
They both had been. Everyone was mad at Lori for
trying to snare him. He didn't know if that were true.
He did know that the idea of getting married so young
had scared him. He was afraid they'd have a kid and
then another until maybe he'd end up robbing a store
out of sheer desperation, just like his father. During
his junior year, he had carried the scholarship offers
around with him, but he had known he wouldn't use
them. He had believed that he'd never get a four-year
degree or come back to wear the uniform. Instead, he
had thought that he'd marry Lori and live on the rez
in public housing and work for the lumber mill or with
the tribe's cattle. His mother and her mother wouldn't
speak to one another. Still didn't. And his mother had
said she would not attend the wedding.

But he had been the one who had driven them out
to the reservoir and afterward let Lori take the fall
for what they had both done. It was his fault as much
as Lori's. That made him most angry of all.

Ty had told him that her older sister had tried to
pin a baby on him because of his reputation, but he'd
been smart enough to never sleep with Jocelyn. Ty
said Joceyln had slept with so many boys in high
school no one knew whose kid it was. Had Lori done
the same to him?

Jake blinked, but his vision remained blurry. He
rubbed his burning eyes and swayed. When had he
last slept?

WHEN LORI CAUGHT Jake weaving with fatigue, she convinced him to sit down at the nurses' station. It was a mistake, because in pressing him into a stool, she felt first the taut muscles that offered resistance, and then the warmth of his skin. Now her palms prickled. But she tore herself away from temptation and brought him something to eat and drink—yogurt, applesauce and orange juice, everything served in tiny clear plastic cups.

"Aren't you tired?" he asked.

"I only came on duty at six a.m."

"I called before six," he said and blinked wearily at her.

"I was early."

"Better than being late." He grinned.

Was that a reference to when she had missed a period and had told him using those very words? She narrowed her eyes on him as her attraction warred with bitter memories.

"Go home, Jake. I can take it from here."

He shook his head, reminding her of a hound. His eyelids drooped, making him look sexy as hell. Her stomach muscles squeezed, and she clamped her jaw against the tingling arousal threading through her body. *Not this man.*

Being seen with Jake Redhorse would only start tongues wagging and again make her a target for mockery. She acknowledged that not acting on the intense jolt of desire that grew with each moment she spent in his company was not the same as not feeling that desire. Lori accepted that her attraction for Jake Redhorse might be ever-present, a condition from which she would never recover. Just like when faced with the common-cold virus, avoidance was the best option.

The longer he hung around, the more difficulty she would have not succumbing to those come-hither stares and his sexy, lazy smile. It tore her up like shards of glass.

His mouth quirked, and she realized she'd been staring, remembering their night together. Had it really been that good?

"Go home, Jake. Seriously."

"Naw," he said at last, pushing his hat far back on his head and yawning. "I'll stay till you hear from Protective Services. I want to be sure she's staying on the rez."

She didn't say that there was a possibility they might take the baby to a different placement. She gnawed on her cuticle.

"I know that look," he said. "You're worried about something."

She lowered her hand from her mouth, flicking the bit of ragged cuticle on her thumbnail with her index finger.

"We've never taken custody of a baby like this one."

"You mean white?"

She nodded. "We keep and place all Apache infants within our tribe, but she has no protection under ICWA."

He nodded, obviously familiar with the Indian

Child Welfare Act, the legislation that sought to keep Indian children in Indian homes in response to the horrific number of indigenous children who had once been adopted away.

"She might be Indian, a member of the Turquoise Canyon tribe."

Lori made a face. "It's possible. Hard to say without knowing the identity of her parents."

He nodded. "Working on that. Until then, I'll stay here to keep an eye on little Fortune."

"Fortune?"

He shrugged. "That's what you called her. Said she was fortunate."

"She's not a puppy we found, Jake. She's a baby. You can't name her."

His face was strained, though from the pain or the subject matter, she didn't know.

"A baby, all right. A baby girl," he said.

Like the one they had lost. Same size, same big blue eyes. But this was not their child. Whose was it?

"When will they be here?" he asked.

"Well, since we're a Safe Haven Provider, they might not even come. May just give us directions by phone."

"But they can't put her in temporary placement until we investigate for a missing child," said Jake.

"She's not missing."

"I agree. Still have to run it through the system, though."

He knew the law. She knew this particular bit, as she had been here when one teen mother appeared at the clinic to relinquish her child. The father had been contacted, and the young man had signed away his rights to his baby before the infant was placed. The Turquoise Canyon tribe had a 100 percent adoption rate of their children. Their tribe's history of losing their youth to the training school that had once taken over the education and raising of Apache boys and girls made the tribe diligent in raising their own children.

In the past, parents did not *have* to agree to send their children, but once their people were resigned to the reservations, they faced a devil's choice. They could keep their children home and lose their government subsidy and the only way to feed their families. Or they could send their children, receive the subsidies but lose the ability to teach their young their language and their heritage. The choice and the deep wound that remained made the tribe fiercely protective of its youth.

"What if she comes back?" he asked. "The mother, I mean."

"She has parental rights," said Lori.

"She shows up here and I arrest her. Glad to. Leaving Fortune out in the wind. Just wrong." He wasn't even using complete sentences now. This was bad.

"She might be young, Jake. Young people don't always make the best decisions."

He met her gaze, knowing the subject of the conversation had shifted.

HE LET THE fatigue drag at him, rounding his shoulders. His ears were ringing.

Jake's head drooped and his words slurred. "Should be out investigating. Find who left her." He gave a dull shake of his head. "Not right."

"Detective Bear Den is at your house. They're investigating."

Which meant he'd drawn their only detective away from his other investigations, including a recent murder, the growing list of runaways and the relocation of the entire tribal headquarters to a temporary facility away from the river. He closed his eyes, swaying slightly on the stool.

"Come on, Officer Redhorse. Bedtime for you."

Lori held his arm as she walked him to an empty birthing room with a comfortable bed and waited while he removed his open jacket and utility belt.

"Want me to lock that up?" Lori asked.

"Where?"

"Right there in the closet." She pointed at the combination bureau and closet unit that backed up to the bathroom near the entrance. He judged the strength of the particle board and figured he could break it if he needed to.

"It's safe," she repeated. "But it's a maternity wing. That—" she pointed at his gun "—needs to be locked up. So here or the nurses' station."

"Here. Leave the key."

She opened the closet and he accepted her help to remove his jacket, mainly to feel her cool fingers brush his neck. Now the ache in his chest had more to do with regret than arousal. She'd taken a lot of crap back in high school, after word got out. It had been worse for her than for him. He didn't know why, but, at the time, he'd been relieved.

He considered taking off his flak jacket but was just too tired.

He sat on the bed and she knelt to unlace his boots, placing them with his jacket, hat and belt. Then she locked the closet and handed him the key on a lime-green plastic accordion-style bracelet that he looped around his wrist.

He settled back into soft pillows and a mattress covered with something plastic beneath the white sheet.

"We'll take care of her," she assured him and stroked his forehead.

He was shaking his head again. "My job."

"Why is it your job?" she asked, smiling down at him.

"Because I found her."

She straightened and drew back, her smile gone. She sighed. "That is not how this works."

"Lori? Does this mean that we're talking again?"

He waited while she blew away a breath and then crossed her arms protectively before her, the shields coming up again.

"Maybe. But it's hard, Jake. When I see you, I remember…"

"Our daughter."

She dropped her chin and nodded.

"Yes, and everything else."

Jake opened his arms and gathered her up as she rested her forehead on his shoulder. She kept her arms crossed but let him hold her, rub her back. He hadn't held her since they'd lost their own baby, and that had not gone well. The time before that had been in his truck. She'd said yes, yes to everything. And that was her fault as much as his.

Lori drew back first, of course, and he let her go. It seemed that was all he ever did.

"I'd like to be able to talk to you, Lori. And not just about what happened."

Her eyes were cautious. She had reason to be suspicious, but not as much reason as he had to be suspicious of her.

"Talk, huh?" She gave him a look that cut through the bull. He wanted many things, but talk wasn't exactly one of them.

She changed the subject, dismissing him and the topic.

"Your captain said you were on patrol last night, that you covered the traffic fatality and who knows what else. So, bed. Now."

He stroked a strand of her hair that had escaped the tight knot. Instead of drawing back, she let him cup her head in his hand. He met her gaze, letting her know what he intended and giving her time to step away.

It was a bad idea, but he was still going for it. No stopping himself, just like the last time they were alone. But he was older now. His control was better.

Liar. She still stripped away all control. There was no containing the fire that burned within him for this woman. His brain shrieked a warning as he pulled her in tight.

Her eyes widened as she sucked in air through flaring nostrils. The small gesture made his chest constrict. He flexed his arm, bringing her in closer. Her fingers slipped into the opening of his uniform at the collar, nails raking his chest. His blood surged and he took the kiss, his mouth hungry. Her arms threaded around his neck as he deepened the kiss, tasting the sweetness of her mouth. She was like a drug for him. The habit he thought to break, and all the while it had lingered inside him, waiting for a chance to have her again. If she had learned anything, she should be running for the door because they were alone again, and there was a bed right beside them.

He turned her in his arms and brought her to the mattress. She stiffened and broke the kiss. He lifted to his elbows to give her a questioning look. She gaped at him and then shoved away, slipping from his grasp. He sat on the bed while she stood panting beside him. He'd dragged the forked comb from the tight bun and let her hair fall. Then he raked his fingers through the strands until her hair fell about her shoulders in soft waves.

"Jake, you can't do that."

But he just had. His mouth quirked.

"That so?"

"Yes, that *is* so, Jake Redhorse. You might be the golden boy to everyone else, but you and I know better. Don't we?" She reclaimed her hair fastener.

That stung. He drummed his fingers on his thigh.

"I said I'd marry you, didn't I?"

She gave a sharp, audible exhale and folded her arms over her chest. "My hero," she said, her tone mocking. Then she spun on her heels and marched out of the room.

He had half a mind to follow her.

Jake flopped back onto the bed. And what was that "my hero" gibe about? She'd gone with him, let him do what he liked. They'd both been there, both been stupid kids. It wasn't his fault. At least not *all* his fault. His mistake had been thinking he could control himself with Lori. He'd even had the damn condom in his pocket. But that wasn't how a condom worked, was it?

He hadn't used protection and she had never asked about it. Thinking a Mott girl would use protection was like expecting a cow to wear pajamas. That was what his brother Ty had said. Kee had said it was an unfortunate but predictable occurrence given family history. The whole thing still made him burn deep inside, shame and hurt and desire all firing at once. But he would admit that whatever appeal Lori had for him had only grown stronger with time.

What was it about Lori Mott that drew him like a lamb to slaughter?

"No," he promised to the empty room and settled down in the bed alone. The pillow smelled like Lori. He breathed deep and then growled, rolling to his side, ignoring the stirring of his body for her.

Not again.

Chapter Four

Lori stomped away to the nurses' station. She was so mad she could spit nickels. She plunged into work, muttering to herself. Officer Redhorse was no white knight. She knew it even if no one else did. But somehow he always came out of every situation smelling like a rose. It burned her up inside.

Did he actually believe what everyone had said about her? He'd been there, for heaven's sake. He knew exactly how it had played out. But in the days and weeks after the miscarriage, Jake had disappeared. Bolted like a branded calf. She'd learned from her older sister Rosa that Jake had been congratulated on his escape.

And she'd just kissed him again. She must be out of her mind. Lori gave Fortune a bottle of formula and brought baby Leniix to her mother for feeding. She spoke to Betty Mills briefly about the new arrival. When she finally felt herself again, she returned to give Jake a piece of her mind and found him puffing softly in slumber. Lori permitted herself the pleasure of looking at the handsome boy who had grown into an even more handsome man. You just couldn't tell from the outside what lay inside. Sometimes you learned that only when it was too late. When her throat began to ache, she crept out.

She was in the women's health clinic with Dr. Redhorse all morning and was called to the urgent-care unit twice when they became swamped. Midmorning, Lori noticed Jake's mother at the clinic, accompanied by her new husband, Duffy Rope. May Redhorse Rope never liked Lori after what had happened and had been strongly in favor of letting the baby go to adoption within the tribe so her precious son would not have to be encumbered by a marriage to the likes of her. When Jake had announced that he planned to marry Lori, May would not speak to her, but she made sure Lori heard what she thought. May's words were engraved in Lori's memory like letters on a tombstone.

He shouldn't have to spend a lifetime tied to a girl like that because of one simple mistake.

Lori and May made eye contact, and May glowered. Lori went to fetch Dr. Kee Redhorse. She didn't need any extra rancor this morning.

She later learned that May had a new ulcer on her foot above her big toe amputation and needed special wound care twice a week. Kee had made an appointment in Darabee with a specialist. Lori did not like Jake's mother, but she would not wish her troubles on anyone.

Dr. Kee left for lunch and Lori ordered in, then returned to the computer to code entries while she waited. They didn't have a proper cafeteria, but they had a break room and a standing arrangement with the diner across the street to have food delivered when needed.

Her order arrived with a familiar deliveryman. Bullis had left the grill to hand-deliver her meal. He'd been after her for months for a date, but she had put him off. He owned the diner and was a nice guy. But he just didn't make her tingle all over—like Officer Redhorse. More was the pity. Nathan was the better choice because he gave her something Jake never had—respect.

"Extra sandwich," said Nathan, lifting a bag. "Roast beef with mustard, lettuce, tomato, with potato salad and a bag of chips. Plus one sixteen-ounce iced tea." He glanced around. "This for Nina? She usually drinks diet."

"No. A, er, visitor. Jake Redhorse. Sleeping in there."

Nathan frowned. "Why?"

News would get out anyway. It always did. "He found a baby in his truck."

"A baby? No way. Can I see it?"

She held her smile and handed over a twenty. "Family only, I'm afraid."

Nathan expertly made change. "Just found it, huh?"

"Yes. She's doing well."

"Ain't that something." He just stood there staring at her, and she felt sure he was going to ask her out yet again.

"Well." She glanced at her computer. "Better get back to work."

Nathan nodded and finally left, looking back only once this time.

Lori resisted the urge to check on Jake, but instead sent Nina to pop her head in. She returned a few minutes later with her report. "Still sleeping. Still cute. I left him a pitcher of ice water by his bed."

Lori sighed as she returned to seeing patients and finished up the afternoon paperwork. The women's health clinic closed at two o'clock on weekdays. The urgent-care unit stayed open until four from Monday to Saturday. After that, the tribe knew to wait until morning or call the volunteer fire department, now relocating until Piñon Forks was safe again. This week was unusual for them, too, because they'd be moving lock, stock and barrel to Turquoise Ridge tomorrow.

Baby Leniix and her mother had been discharged, leaving only baby Fortune, as Lori was now thinking of her. Lori and Nina packed boxes until nearly six.

"I'm going to wake up Officer Redhorse and see about getting him home," said Lori.

"Okay," said Nina, casting her a smile that showed much pink gum above her teeth before she returned to the computer and the records.

Lori retrieved the bag lunch and carried it to the room where Jake rested.

The golden September sunlight stretched across Jake's bare arm and chest. At some point he'd removed his vest and his shirt now flapped open, giving her an eyeful of his heavily muscled torso. Her breath caught and she worried her lip as she considered turning tail.

Instead, she stepped closer.

You can do this, she thought. *He's just a man. Like every other man.* But he wasn't. He was the one man who short-circuited all her wiring, and he did it while asleep. That irritated her, but not enough to tamp down the unrest. She clenched the fist of her free hand to keep herself from stroking down the centerline of his body.

She stared at him, her body as tense as his was relaxed. It was safe now, since he was asleep.

But it wasn't. Not really. Lori stretched her fingers and reached, unable to stop herself. She only just managed to redirect her touch to his forearm. His muscles twitched as her fingertips registered warm skin and the texture of the dark hair. His eyes flashed open as he reached with his opposite hand to his hip where his gun usually sat.

"It's me," she said and stepped away, clutching the bag before her.

The tension left his body. He squeezed his eyes shut, scrubbing his closed lids with his fingertips before forcing his eyes open again.

"Sorry. You startled me."

He pushed himself to a sitting position, and her gaze slipped to his abdomen and the ribbed muscle there. She swallowed down the gnawing hunger.

"Everything all right?" he asked.

"Yes." She forced her gaze upward to his face. Thankfully, he was looking toward the hallway.

"Who's with Fortune?"

"Nina."

He nodded and scrubbed his hands over his face.

His shirt flapped opened, giving her an unimpeded look at flexing chest muscles as he stretched. Her throat went dry and her eyes widened. He was making her sweat and he'd barely looked at her.

He noticed the water and poured a plastic cup full. She watched in silence as his Adam's apple bobbed with each long swallow. Her stomach fluttered and she closed her gaping mouth.

She resisted the urge to step closer. *Oh, no, you don't*, she told herself.

He wiped his wet lips with the back of his hand and then met her gaze. Did he see the raw desire there?

Jake's mouth quirked. "What time is it?"

She glanced at her watch. "A little after six."

His brows lifted. "Really? Seven solid hours. Can't believe it."

No one had gotten much sleep since the dam collapse. Everyone at the clinic was working long hours. They'd stayed open around the clock for the first three days to treat all the injuries resulting from the explosion and evacuation.

His gaze dipped and her skin flushed as his eyes roamed over her body and then settled on the bag she had forgotten she held.

"Do I smell food?" he asked.

She nodded and dropped the bag onto the mobile table. In a moment she had the table wheeled in place beside the bed, automatically adjusting the level to suit him. He ignored the food and instead stared at her.

She didn't know what to do with her hands. Should she leave him to eat or stay? Lori glanced toward the corridor with longing.

Despite how it had ended, Jake had been kind to her after he got over the shock. He'd also stood by her and defended her from his mother, who'd opposed the marriage so vehemently. Her mother had been for it, delighted, in fact. But things had changed after she'd lost their baby. The distance between them had yawned as they drifted further and further apart. Lori laced her hands across her flat stomach, feeling a hollow ache that reached all the way to her heart.

"Any word from Bear Den?" asked Jake.

Lori shook her head. "No one from the force has been here all day."

Silence stretched as the tension between them crackled like ice cubes meeting water. Jake pushed away the table that separated them and rose to his feet. Lori's brain signaled danger, but the message never reached her motor centers because she remained frozen in place. Jake lifted a hand and gently cradled her elbow.

There was a knock, and Lori glanced up to see Dr. Kee Redhorse standing in the door with his perpetual generous grin and warm brown eyes. He'd been in the clinic much of the afternoon.

"So Sleeping Beauty is finally awake," said Kee. "Doesn't seem to have improved your looks any."

He strode in and gave his brother's shoulder a firm pat.

"Anything happen while I was out?" asked Jake.

"Had a few more injuries related to cleanup. Seeing those every day since the explosion. Today it was Lawrence Kesselman."

Lori had helped close the gash on Mr. Kesselman's leg. The man had been gaunt, with deep circles under his eyes. Lori knew the reason. His daughter, Maggie, had run away last Sunday.

"And our mom was in," said Kee. "She's got another sore on her foot."

The men shared a silent exchange that Lori read as worry. May was still able to walk, but if the ulcer did not heal, her condition could change.

"I've been with patients all day except for lunch over at the diner. Not sure which is bigger news, that you two found a baby or that Lori will finally speak to you again."

"Speak to *me*?" Jake sounded incredulous.

She narrowed her eyes at the implication that he'd had reason to avoid verbal exchange with her. If he said another word on the topic, she was going to finally tell him what a complete jerk he was. Why had she let him kiss her?

Lori wouldn't marry him now if he got down on his belly and groveled in the dirt. Redhorse was off the menu and he was not stealing any more kisses, either. Not today or ever.

"Whatever you say, Officer," said Kee, and he gave Jake a playful push.

Jake's mouth twisted as he allowed the shove to rock him and did not offer an insult back as he was likely to do with Ty or Colt. Kee had always been treated differently because of his leg-length discrepancy. His younger brothers looked out for him, his fiercest defenders. Even now, after the corrective surgery, the Redhorse men persisted as if their eldest still required special handling.

"How did Lawrence look?" asked Jake, wisely changing the subject.

"Just as you're imagining."

"Bear Den had me do that initial interview with him."

"A tough place to start. A missing child, I mean."

Jake did not disagree. "He also had me check back with the families of the others. A follow-up interview."

"What others?" asked Kee.

"We have five missing girls since last November."

"What? I didn't know that," said Kee. "Who?"

Jake listed the names, and Kee's frown deepened. He turned to Lori. "Didn't we see Maggie here last week?"

"I'm not sure," she said. But the hairs on her arms were lifting as she considered the possibility. She was not sure about Maggie. But she was positive they had recently seen two of the other girls Jake had just mentioned.

"What's wrong, Lori?" asked Jake.

"Maybe nothing. Excuse me, gentlemen."

She stepped out, leaving Jake and Kee to watch her abrupt exit.

"What was that about?" asked Kee.

"Don't know."

"So…" Kee rocked back and forth from heel to toe. "You two back together?"

Jake's reply was way too fast and way too angry. "No way."

"Really? Because when I got here, I thought I was interrupting."

"That was nothing."

"Seemed like something. All I know is that no one here has gotten more than a second date with Ms. Mott, and Nathan Bullis has been trying for weeks. At least he got her out once. I haven't even managed that much."

"You asked Lori Mott out on a date?" Jake stared at his brother as if he had told him that he had been picked for the mission to Mars.

"More than once."

"Why?"

Kee laughed and then frowned as he saw his brother was not joking.

"Ty told me that both Jocelyn and Amelia Mott tried to snag you in high school," said Jake.

"Not exactly," said Kee and grinned. "Amelia got in trouble with a boy." He shrugged. "It happens."

Jake's gaze darted away and then quickly back as he anticipated the censure in Kee's expression. But he saw only the gentle acceptance Kee always gave him.

The same situation had happened to Jake in high school and he knew exactly the kind of contained panic Kent Haskie must have experienced. Kee did not draw the obvious comparison but instead filled the awkward pause.

"Amelia was just a scared kid and the boy she was seeing, Kent Haskie, wouldn't marry her. I just went out with her a time or two. Then Kurt Bear Den took her to the Autumn dance. That really helped convince Haskie to get past his fear and see that he loved Amelia. Now I treat her kids. She's a great mom and she and Kurt seem very happy."

"That is not at all how Ty tells it," said Jake. "What about Jocelyn?"

"What about her?"

"She tried to get you to go out with her, too."

"No. Never. She spoke to me about Amelia's situation. Then I came up with the idea to take Amelia out a few times. That was all."

Jake rubbed his neck, wondering if Ty's perception could really have been so wrong.

"But regardless, Lori is not her sisters," said Kee.

"What's that even mean?"

Kee cocked his head and his brows lowered as if also confused. "She works outside the home, for one thing. She has an education, for another, and is very good at what she does." Kee began ticking off Lori's attributes on his fingers. "Well, she's beautiful, of course, and smart, funny and, most of all, kind. Oh, and you should see her with babies. She's a natural. Would make a great mother."

Jake did not like Kee's Cheshire grin.

"Bet she'd love to snag a doctor."

Kee snorted. "Well, not this one, anyway."

"Why'd she say no?"

Kee lifted his brows. "You like being judged by

what our father has done? Or by what Ty's done? By your logic, then, we're all criminals with gang ties."

Jake had worked particularly hard to keep that from happening. He was *not* his father. Jake scowled now and faced his brother, who was three inches shorter since the corrective surgery.

"It's not the same," Jake said, but his argument felt forced now.

"No?" said Kee. "I think it's exactly the same, except I'm not simultaneously carrying a torch and a grudge like you. But Lori said that she doesn't date where she works, and she said she had sworn off Redhorse men. Thanks a lot, brother."

"Maybe she's just playing hard to get."

"You really are delusional, you know?"

"What are you talking about?"

"She's not sixteen anymore. Neither are you, and Lori is a registered nurse with a good job and no student loans, which is more than I can say for myself. She's taking night classes to become a midwife. When she finishes that, she can deliver those babies all on her own. She'll be in high demand, will deserve a raise, and we'll be darn lucky to keep her."

"But…" His arguments stalled.

Kee poked him with an extended index finger. "And she makes a better salary than you do. I know what we pay her, and you're a public servant, so your salary goes right in the newspaper. Plus, I find it insulting that you think the only things about me that would appeal to a woman are my position and income."

"Don't get all defensive."

"I may be three inches shorter than all of you, but my perspective on Lori is better than yours. And if she looked at me the way she looks at you, I wouldn't be pushing her away."

"Looking like she hates me, you mean."

"Did you or did you not kiss her today?"

"How do you know that?"

Kee lifted one finger and pointed at Jake's upper lip. "Raspberry lip gloss."

Jake swiped the back of his hand over his mouth.

"Better question is, if you think she's a mantrap, why are *you* kissing her?"

Chapter Five

Lori used a search engine to find the dates of the disappearances of the five girls. Then she used the tribe's medical records to access the dates of patient appointments. A disturbing pattern emerged. Each lost teen had been seen at the clinic a few days before they went missing, except the first, Elsie Weaver. Her appointment had been over a month before she vanished and she had no follow-up. The others, however, had disappeared within one to three days of their visits. Lori scowled at the list of dates. That was a big coincidence.

She studied the records. Elsie had fractured her right wrist. Maggie had lice.

Lori continued to scan. Kacey had come in for a physical for college admission. Brenda had been treated for ringworm. Marta had her first gynecologic appointment due to heavy menstruation and cramping. Marta had been given a prescription for iron supplements due to anemia. All these girls except Elsie had a follow-up nearly a month after their first appointments, which was unusual in itself. They were seen for a follow-up and then…disappeared.

Something odd was happening. Did this all have anything to do with the eco-extremists who'd taken out their dam? Did the missing girls run, or were they taken?

"You still here?"

Lori startled clean out of her seat and to her feet at the unexpected appearance of her supervisor. Usually Lori heard Betty clicking down the hallway long before she appeared. But her supervisor now stood before the raised counter that surrounded the nurses' station on three sides, looking down her thin nose at Lori. Betty was middle-aged, divorced and wore clothing that showed her trim figure to good advantage. She favored bright blouses that revealed the many fine gold chains encircling her neck.

Lori forced a smile. "Oh, Betty."

"Did I scare you? What are you working on?" Betty leaned over the desk but was too short to see the screen.

Lori moved the mouse and clicked. The database was replaced with the coding page for her most recent patients.

"You know…" Lori's laugh seemed artificial and tinny. "Just coding."

Betty's smile was tight. "From the way you jumped, I thought it was porn."

Lori's face went hot.

"Who is coming in after you?"

"Nobody. I called Burl and told him I'd cover it."

If they had any babies in the nursery, they worked nights; otherwise they worked one hour past closing.

Betty nodded at this. "I'm leaving. Just wanted to get another look at that baby you found." Betty turned to the viewing area to look at their one charge. Fortune slept alone in the nursery. Her supervisor spoke over her shoulder. "Any word yet from Child Protective Services?"

"No." Lori frowned. That was odd.

Betty cocked her head, and one of her plucked and penciled brows quirked.

"Let me give them another jingle. You need anything before I go?"

Lori told her she did not and waited until Betty was out of sight to press her hand to her chest and sag on her stool.

Why hadn't she told her supervisor what she had discovered? That would have been the perfect opportunity.

Lori glanced around the quiet floor. If there was a connection between the missing girls and the tribe's health care clinic, then someone here already knew. But who?

It could be anyone she worked with here. She ran through the names of the other nurses—Nina Kenton, Burl Tsosie and Verna Dia, their administrator, Betty Mills, and the two doctors, Hector Hauser and Kee Redhorse. Other than that, they had cleaning staff, but they would not have access to medical records. At least, she didn't believe they would.

She headed off to see Jake, her earlier rancor overcome by her concern that something was going on here. She stopped in the nursery and lifted the sleeping baby Fortune, then carried her out to the room where Jake rested.

Lori found the room empty and the bathroom door closed. She could hear him humming. She knocked and the humming stopped.

"It's Lori. I need to speak to you."

This was met with momentary silence and then Jake called that he'd be right out. The door opened to a billow of steam and Jake standing in only his uniform trousers with a white hospital towel wrapped around his neck and that charming grin on his face. He held the towel with both hands at his chest, which made his biceps bulge. Lori gaped.

"I'm sorry, Lori, for what I said before. I was out of line."

His wet hair clung to his shoulders in dark strands, and Lori could only gawk.

"It was a bad time. Bad memories."

Some were bad and others wonderful. Had it been all bad for him? No, she knew better. That night in his truck? That had been real, and he had been as affected as she had been. His mask of the small-tribe hero had slipped and he'd been there, had let her see inside to the pain and the hope warring within him.

His gaze slipped to her shoulder. "Is that Fortune?"

He stepped close, moving so he could see her little sleeping face. "No mask?" he asked.

"We've both already exposed her to whatever

we're breathing, and I didn't want to leave her alone in the nursery."

She remembered another time she'd held a newborn baby with him here. They'd sent him in because she would not let them take their baby from her.

"Go on, take her," she'd shouted at him, holding out their baby. "It's what they sent you in here to do. But don't come back, because I never want to see you again."

It shamed her, that outburst. How her pain and grief had spilled out on him.

He turned his troubled eyes from her to Fortune. Then he made a sound in his throat that made her stomach tighten. He smelled like soap, and she could feel the heat and dampness of his skin. The sight of his hand on Fortune's head caused Lori's skin to flush and her breathing to increase. He was doing it to her again. Always. The man was like catnip to a house tabby. She was drunk with the sight and smell of him when he finally stepped back.

"What's up?" he asked.

Retreat was the logical option. Lori made it to the chair by the window in his room, and he followed. He lifted the undershirt from his bed.

"I had a shower. Hope that's all right. Need some coffee," he muttered.

"Nurses' station," she said, and her voice shook.

His brows sank. "You okay?"

"Not really. No."

Jake drew on his T-shirt, and her brain began to reengage. She started talking as he dressed, dragging on his body armor and buttoning his uniform shirt. When she got to the part about the dates corresponding to the disappearances, he clipped on his utility belt and adjusted the position of his service weapon.

"Could be a coincidence," he said, but his expression said otherwise.

"I sure hope so."

"I'm calling Bear Den."

"Come on, I'll get you some coffee."

He followed her out and back to the nurses' station, where he poured a cup of black coffee and made the call.

Jake disconnected shortly afterward and looked long and hard at Lori. "He's finally made it back to my house to check the crime scene."

"What took so long?"

"He was on another call, a domestic dispute. Had to make an arrest and process the suspect. Get the witness statement and the wife to agree to press charges."

It happened more often than it should, Lori thought.

"He wants me to meet him there."

Why did that make Lori feel anxious? She worked nights alone here all the time, and up until this minute, she'd enjoyed the quiet and the babies. Now the clinic had taken on a sinister feel. She met Jake's stare. He didn't look happy.

"Lori, I don't want you staying here alone with Fortune until we know what's going on."

"I don't have the authority to remove her from the clinic."

"Well, you can't call Hauser or my brother for authority, since they might be connected to the missing girls."

Had he just said that? How could Jake so easily consider his oldest brother a suspect of some crime?

"Girls are disappearing, Jake. Not babies. We've never lost a baby here."

He made a face.

"She stays here, Jake. In the nursery with everything we need for her care, along with locks and key cards so she's safe."

His hands went to his hips. "Fine. Then I'm staying, too."

JAKE LEFT LORI only to accept delivery of a pizza and two liters of soda. He returned with a large cheese-and-sausage—and Detective Bear Den.

Bear Den was a giant of a man, and Lori had heard gossip that he was not actually Turquoise Canyon, but a mix of Apache and Hawaiian. It accounted for the wave in his hair and the width of his shoulders.

Bear Den asked for the dates, and she provided him with the folded sheet of paper on which she had written the dates of the visits of the missing girls, knowing that releasing medical records was a violation of patients' rights and could get her fired. He was a detective and this was related to a case. Still, she was getting deeper and deeper into trouble. This happened every time she got near Jake Redhorse.

"Don't mention this connection to anyone, especially not the clinic staff," Bear Den said to Lori. Then he turned to Jake. "That includes your brother Kee."

"I understand," Jake said.

The men stepped down the hall to speak in private. Fortune woke hungry and wet, and Lori was consumed with taking care of the baby until Jake returned alone, his phone pressed to his ear. She buzzed him into the nursery area and heard the message he left for his brother Ty, which surprised her. The relationship between the former gang member and his little brother had been rocky since Jake announced his intention to join the police academy. Had they made amends?

He put his phone in one of the many pockets of his uniform and came to check on the baby.

"Did they figure out where the mother went?" she asked.

"No. That's why I called Ty. He's got that dog. She's a good tracker."

Lori knew that dog. It went everywhere with Ty. The female was big and black with a collar of fur like a wolf.

"You sure that's a dog?" she asked.

"German shepherd and husky mix."

Lori made a sound in her throat and set the sleeping baby back in her bassinet. "If you say so."

The awkward silence stretched. She shifted, fiddling with the pencils in the metal cylinder on the desk.

"Don't you have to go in to work tonight?" she asked.

His mouth quirked. "Trying to get rid of me?"

"No." Her words sounded less than convincing, even to her own ears.

"Tonight *this* is my work. You and Fortune." He turned toward the newborn and she followed. They stood a minute, shoulder to shoulder, gazing down at her face, the round cheeks, tiny nose and soft wisp of blond hair. She yawned, and they both chuckled.

"They are amazing," said Lori.

"Babies?"

She nodded and slipped a hand into the crook of his arm, leaning her head on his shoulder. The muscle there was firm and inviting.

"Did you feed her?" asked Jake, reaching his free hand to stroke the baby's pink cheek with one finger.

"Yes." She lifted her head from his shoulder to offer him a smile. "She has a good appetite."

He looked tentative now as he directed his attention to her. "Do you think I could feed her sometime?"

"Of course." They always had the fathers feed the babies at the clinic. It helped form a bond. But helping Jake form a bond with this baby was dangerous, because he couldn't keep her unless he was the father. Lori's smile faltered. Jake wasn't the father. Her eyes widened.

Was he?

It would explain why the infant had been left in his truck. Lori released Jake's arm and stepped back.

"Jake, is that your baby?"

JAKE TOSSED ON the couch in the lounge most of the night, listening for Fortune's cry and wondering if Lori was sleeping any better than he was. He'd slept too long in the afternoon after his sixteen-hour shift to be able to sleep well now and had been up both times she heated formula, standing at the window like a new father until she buzzed him in. He held Fortune while she cried in hunger and returned her to Lori to be fed.

His pride still stung at her question. You could tell by just looking at the newborn that he wasn't the father. He wasn't a geneticist, but he was fairly certain a brown-skinned man with black hair was not likely to have a baby who looked like she'd been dropped by a Norwegian stork. Jake could not believe Lori had leaped to that conclusion.

But why not? He'd gotten her pregnant, and this baby had been left with him. Jake believed the mother wanted to be certain the infant was protected, and so she'd left her with a police officer. But protected from what, or whom?

He had convinced Lori that this wasn't his child, but he found the entire discussion disturbing. He had not had a steady woman since high school, when he and Alice Ybarra had broken up and he'd asked Lori out. Since nearly becoming a father, Jake had been much more cautious than other men his age. Trouble was, he wanted to be a father. But he wanted a woman he could trust and who trusted him. Lori Mott was not that woman. So why was he fantasizing about seeing her naked? He closed his eyes and breathed deeply, imagining the light floral scent of her, picturing her beneath him on this lumpy couch.

Dinner had been awkward. Caring for Fortune had been the only thing that felt natural. He shouldn't have kissed her. But the truth was, he had never gotten over Lori. He'd gone out with Alice Ybarra because everyone expected him to. She was class president and the lead in every play they'd ever staged, and he was the school's point guard and captain of the basketball and track teams four years running. It wasn't until Alice found out about the baby that she showed her true colors. Jake did not want a woman with a mean spirit. It had been Alice who told everyone that the pregnancy had been Lori's fault. And he'd done nothing to shoulder the blame that was more than half his.

Why was it that women were called vile names and men congratulated for doing exactly the same thing? And as for the pregnancy, he'd gotten sympathy. But not Lori. Sympathy was not the reaction of her classmates. They weren't surprised, and they were not kind. Not at all. He got so he half believed their version of the truth. Or, at least, he had wanted to believe it.

He was still hurt and raw over what had happened between them, but the attraction that had drawn them together all those years ago was still alive and well. She made his skin tingle and his body twitch. His body affected her, too. He saw it. But she was either angry at him or just not willing to deal with all their problems.

Jake threw off the thin hospital blanket she'd offered him, giving up on the notion of sleep. The sun would be up soon, he thought, and then he checked his phone to confirm his suspicion. He walked down the darkened hall on stocking feet and visited the restroom to wash up, then adjusted his rumpled uniform.

He ventured out to the viewing window, gazing in to notice that Fortune was out of her bassinet. He found Lori in the rocker set inside the nursery. She held Fortune naturally to her chest so that the baby's cheek nestled against the bare skin at her neck. He took in the picture they made, mother and child, the images that he had only kept in his heart until now made suddenly real.

The corridor lights flicked on, and Jake turned to see a large man in scrubs heading toward him.

"Good morning, Officer Redhorse."

Jake recognized Burl Tsosie, who smiled broadly. The man was the only male nurse at the clinic. That— and his size—made him the go-to person for moving patients. Lori had mentioned that she was only supposed to work until six last night, but she'd stayed over, as well.

"How are you, Burl?"

"Great! Lori told me I didn't need to come in last night. So I'm well rested. More than I can say for you."

"You're early, aren't you?"

"Yeah. I was up. Moving day. The boxes are here. I saw them on my way in."

Burl had a fleshy face, broad shoulders and a paunch. He wore blue scrubs, white sneakers and a wide grin. Like Lori, Burl's long, dark hair was pulled back, but his in a single ponytail. He knew Burl was slightly older than him and Lori, but his hairline was receding at an alarming rate.

"I heard you had some excitement yesterday."

Did Burl mean the auto accident or the baby?

"Yeah."

"Someone just left her in your truck? Have you found the mother yet?"

"Not yet."

"Can't understand it. Who doesn't love babies?"

Jake thought of his sixteen-year-old self and knew the answer.

"Well, I'll go make a fresh pot of coffee," Burl said.

Jake returned to the lounge to retrieve his shoes. He was sitting on the couch, tying his laces, when something pelted the window. At first he thought it was ice, but it stopped immediately. He walked to the window.

The sun was still an hour or so from making an appearance, so it was darker outside the clinic than inside. Another scattering of sand and pebbles hit the window. He pressed his face to the glass and peered out. It took a moment for his eyes to adjust to the light of the setting half-moon.

Something dark jumped up on the window. Jake leaped back, hand going to his pistol as he saw two large paws and the glowing green eyes of an animal.

Chapter Six

"Hemi!" Jake exclaimed, recognizing his brother's dog. Jake swore and then turned to retrieve his hat and jacket. He was outside the clinic a moment later.

The dog reached him first, her nose pressing to Jake's trousers. Jake rubbed her head and spoke to the dog.

"Hemi," he said, his tone admonishing. "You nearly scared me to death."

The dog cocked her head and retreated, quiet as a moving shadow.

Folks said she looked like a wolf, but that wasn't right. Hemi had none of the lanky hangdog posture of wild creatures. She was big and black, making her nearly invisible at night. But in the predawn, Jake could see her until she reached the row of bushes that lined the landscaped area between the clinic and road. Hemi was bold, but she couldn't throw rocks against a window.

"Ty?"

From somewhere out in the darkness came the reply. "Got your message." Then Ty materialized from the landscape, quiet as his dog.

Jake glanced back to the clinic and then to his brother.

"How did you know I was still here?"

Ty swept a hand toward Jake's police unit, which was parked in the lot. Ty would have made a very good police officer.

"What's up?" His older brother had grown blunter since he returned from the US Marines. He lived at his shop and did not spend time with Jake anymore. He missed his brother.

"I need a favor," said Jake.

"That so?" Ty waited.

Jake looked from his tank of a dog back to Ty. "I found a baby."

"Skip to the part I don't know, like what you want."

Jake remembered a time when Ty used to be his big brother in the figurative sense of the word. Ty had looked out for him, protecting him from bigger kids until he could protect himself. Kee and Ty, the yin and yang of his boyhood. Kee taught Jake how to carve, and Ty showed him how to throw a knife. Kee taught him how to build a sweat lodge; Ty showed him how to set things on fire. Kee taught him how to feed a squirrel out of your hand; Ty taught him how to skin one. Ty had also taught him how to drive and how to play basketball. Ty was the better player, but academics and sports had not been enough to keep him in high school for a minute longer than necessary.

"We can't find the mother. There's blood on the gate of my truck. The mother's blood. I thought you could use it to track her."

"Far as the road, maybe. She's white, right?"

"Seems so." How did Ty know that? He wanted to ask but was somehow afraid to know.

"Start at your truck, right?" asked Ty.

"Yes. Thank you, Ty."

He snorted and turned away.

"How's Colt?"

"Surviving. Doesn't talk."

"Did he tell you what happened over there?"

Ty shook his head and looked at his boots.

"Can I see him?" asked Jake.

Ty glanced at him over his shoulder. "You tried already, didn't you?"

"Yes. I did. A few times."

"Then you can't."

Jake sighed. He wanted to help his little brother, Colt. He didn't think it was healthy for him to stay all alone in that miner's cabin up on Turquoise Ridge.

Ty took a few steps away and paused.

"Keep trying," he said. Then he walked away into the gloom toward the lot. Jake saw the cab light of his truck flash on as Ty held the door for Hemi and then shut it again. A few moments later, Ty was behind the wheel and driving away.

"Quiet truck," he muttered to no one in particular and headed back inside.

Jake was still thinking about his troubled relationship with Ty and was afraid that one day he'd be called on to arrest his brother. Ty had once been arrested but had managed to avoid jail time thanks to enlistment in the US Marines.

He had to call Lori to get back into the clinic. Burl appeared at the door a few moments later and let him in.

"We have two hours of peace before the patients and doctors arrive," said Burl.

He followed Burl back to the women's health wing and the nursery. Burl used his card to let Jake into the nursery, where Lori was wiping down the changing table.

Fortune now lay in her crib, staring up with wide blue eyes.

"Not sleeping?" he asked Lori.

"Not yet."

Fortune yawned and her eyes blinked. Her lids lowered, and the tiny pale lashes brushed her cheeks. The ringing of Jake's cellular phone caused her eyes to open wide, and then her brow wrinkled as she began to cry.

"I'm changing that ringtone to Brahms's 'Lullaby,'" he said and drew out his phone. "Redhorse," he said into it. "Yes." His expression flashed from surprise to worry, and he met Lori's gaze.

What? she mouthed.

He shook his head. "You want us to come in or wait?…Fine. See you then." He disconnected and looked at her.

"What?"

"Chief Tinnin is on his way over. He wants to talk to us both."

"Why?"

"I don't know. He didn't say."

"Did they find the mother?"

Chief Wallace Tinnin stood before Jake and Lori in the break room of the tribe's health clinic. The chief had given up trying to walk with just a cane and now leaned on a pair of ancient wooden crutches that were missing both handgrips. Lori did not know the chief well, but you would have to be blind to miss the look of displeasure in the hard lines of his face.

"You both know it is your responsibility to call Child Protective Services when an infant is recovered," he said.

"Yes, of course. It's part of my training," said Lori.

"So why didn't you call?" he asked.

"Excuse me?"

"The call to Protective Services. It was never placed."

"What? That's impossible. Betty told me she called."

Tinnin straightened. "Well, your supervisor told me that it was only when she called this morning that she discovered you had not contacted Protective Services."

"But she said..." Lori scrambled to recall the exchange. Had she misunderstood?

"Your training includes procedure for intake of recovered children. Isn't it your duty to call?"

It was. Why hadn't Lori done so? Was it because deep down in her heart she didn't want to let this baby go?

"I made a mistake."

Tinnin nodded. "Yes, ma'am. You sure did."

He turned to Jake. "And so did you. You have a legal obligation to call CPS. Yet neither of you did so."

Lori tapped her teeth together in a nervous staccato.

Tinnin aimed a finger at Jake. "You are getting a verbal warning." Then he lifted his brows and glanced at Lori. "You, Ms. Mott, are getting a formal reprimand from your supervisor. She also told me you should not be here when she arrives in—" he glanced at his watch "—twenty minutes."

Lori nodded her understanding. "Yes, sir."

"She'll let you know when you are meeting with her. You are to stay home until then. If Protective Services wishes to see you, she will let you know."

Lori locked her teeth together until they squeaked, not trusting herself to speak.

"That's all, Ms. Mott. You can go."

Lori cast Jake a quick look and then charged from the room.

Jake watched her go, wishing he could follow. Then he turned to Tinnin. "Did you speak to Detective Bear Den about what Lori uncovered about the missing girls?"

Tinnin nodded. "Doesn't explain why neither of you did your jobs."

"We have protected that infant since she came in here."

"Son, we find babies every year. Most of them aren't as lucky as that little one. We don't post guards around them. That's what this clinic is for. So we can look out for abandoned babies, along with the ones fortunate enough to have someone on this earth who wants them."

"I want her," he said.

"What's that now?" said the chief.

"I want that baby girl."

Tinnin pushed back his hat. "You know what you're doing?"

Jake nodded.

"Well, not saying the tribe would give you that baby, but supposing they did, you'd get six weeks' leave to care for her. What will you do after that?"

"My mother could watch her."

"Your mother, who was none too pleased the last time you were expecting a baby."

"This is different."

Tinnin laughed. "It sure is. This baby is white, and it's not yours." Tinnin's smile vanished and his brows lifted as he pinned his stare on Jake.

"She's not mine," Jake confirmed.

Tinnin's cheeks puffed out as he blew away a breath. "Right, then."

"She's not mine yet. But I'm not leaving her in this clinic."

"Why?"

Jake pressed his lips together and shook his head. He couldn't explain it. Finally, he lifted his hands, palms out, before him. "Just feels wrong."

Tinnin thought about that. "I set a great store by gut feelings, son."

Chapter Seven

Lori had twenty minutes to gather up her things and get out before her supervisor arrived. Instead, she used her key to access the nursery and placed Fortune in one of the baby carriers they lent out to new parents. She knew what Betty had told her, and yes, she should have called Protective Services herself, but Mills had lied to Tinnin. Her short list of people involved with the girls seen at the clinic had just gotten shorter.

Lori retreated behind the nurses' station, where she collected one of their laptops Burl had packed in a box.

Burl was loading supplies into boxes, and he paused to give her a curious look.

"What's up?"

"I need a minute."

Burl glanced at the baby, bundled in a carrier and ready for travel.

"I'll watch her," he said, but his smile was now forced and his eyes were cold.

"Burl, really. Just give me five minutes."

He let his smile drop and rose slowly to his feet.

He was a big man. They faced off. "You can't take her out of here."

"I know that."

"Then why is she in that?"

Lori said nothing. How could she quickly explain the unease and the suspicion in a way that he would accept?

Burl sighed. "Betty called me and told me not to let you near that baby."

"Five minutes."

He glanced around. "Fine. Then you are going to tell me what the heck is happening."

"I will. I swear."

Lori retreated into the utility room with Fortune in a baby carrier looped around one arm and the laptop in the other. Once tucked behind the utility closet door, she placed Fortune on the table, and then she did something she had never done before. She locked the door.

The laptop took forever to boot up as she stood amid the stacked boxes, each labeled for transport. Her fingers flashed as she logged in. In a few minutes, she had a list of all the girls who had come to the clinic for pregnancy tests in the last two years, all the women under twenty-one who'd been seen at the clinic since it opened and all the medical records of each missing girl. She compared the pregnancy-test list to the names of girls who had disappeared since last November and found no matches.

But Lori knew girls ran away for a lot of reasons, and you didn't need to come to a clinic to figure out you were pregnant. Had they each discovered themselves with child and decided to run rather than face their families?

Once, she had considered doing just that. At the time it seemed easier than facing everyone and proving herself to be exactly what they all expected.

There had been no word from any of the missing. That was unusual and disturbing. The girls either would not or could not contact their friends and families.

Lori scanned the medical records of the missing. Elsie Weaver had disappeared in November, followed by Marta Garcia, age sixteen, in February. Also in February was Kacey Doka, age eighteen, and in May, Brenda Espinoza, who was seventeen. Finally, last Monday, Maggie Kesselman had been listed as missing. She was the youngest of the group at fifteen, but not too young to get tangled up with a boy. Lori knew that firsthand.

Two of the girls were from Koun'nde and two from Piñon Forks. Only Maggie was from Turquoise Ridge. In other words, the girls would not necessarily have all known one another. Why did the police think the disappearances might be related?

Lori double-checked the dates of the girls' appointments and confirmed her earlier discovery. All of the girls had been recent patients at the clinic.

Lori opened the mail program and emailed the records to herself, knowing she was now guilty of a violation far more grievous than failing to call Child Protective Services. This one wouldn't get her a reprimand. It would get her fired.

She glanced at her watch. She'd been in here more

than twenty minutes. Mills was likely on her way to see that Lori had been turned out.

There was a bang beyond the locked door, as if someone had knocked over a stainless-steel cart. Lori closed the laptop and stood. Then she lifted Fortune from the table, moved to the door and switched off the light. She pressed an ear to the door. Burl was shouting. There was another voice, low and muffled. Burl's voice was clear.

"You can't go in there!"

Lori's heart pounded as she lifted her phone and called Jake. He picked up on the second ring, still speaking to someone. His chief, she figured.

"Redhorse," he said.

Did he not want Tinnin to know it was her?

"Jake. Something is happening outside the nursery. There was a banging sound, and Burl is yelling at someone."

His voice revealed nothing. "Your location?"

She told him.

"En route," he said, and the line went dead.

THE STAFF ROOM was midway between the urgent-care area and the women's health unit. Jake left the room at a run, leaving Tinnin to gather his crutches and follow.

Jake tore down the hall, outdistancing Tinnin. He'd been the point guard for the high school basketball team and had speed and stamina. When he heard Burl yelling, he drew his pistol.

"Hey! You two! Stop!"

Jake rounded the corner that led to the nurses'

station and saw the shotgun pointed at him. He dived toward the counter and slid on his side all the way to the solid barrier as the shotgun blast peppered the wall behind him with buckshot.

He could imagine Lori cowering behind the door to his left.

Jake glanced back and saw Tinnin pressed against the wall, crutches abandoned and pistol drawn.

"Don't come out!" he yelled.

"I won't," answered Burl from the other side of the nurses' station.

Another blast took out a chunk of the counter above his head.

He prayed the shotgun was a two-shot and not a pump-action as he prepared to make his move. Jake darted up and spotted the shooter half inside the nursery door, beside the overturned cart. Pump-action, he realized.

A woman in the nursery with a bandanna across her face moved from one empty bassinet to another, gripping a swipe card in her hand.

"She's not here!" she yelled.

The gunman yelled, "Let's go!"

"Drop it!" ordered Jake, drawing the shooter's attention.

The gunman did not drop his weapon but primed the pump, sending the next cartridge into the shotgun as Jake ducked back behind the high counter. He was not shooting into a nursery until he knew for certain that Fortune was not there.

The next blast hit above him, the nurses' station

taking the majority of it. The smell of gunpowder and the haze of gray smoke hung in the air above him.

Tinnin fired two shots.

Jake heard footfalls.

"Getting away!" yelled Tinnin.

Jake came around the protection of the barrier between himself and the shooter to find the hallway empty. The same door that Burl had used to admit him earlier banged open.

He reached it a few instants later and saw two suspects, one small and one large, jump into a truck parked on the lawn just past the door, in prime location for a quick retreat.

The engine roared and the pickup tires spun, throwing dirt and sand in Jake's face as he lifted his pistol and fired twice. He wiped at the stinging sand, unable to see. Tinnin hopped through the door, swearing as he went. Jake lowered his hand as Tinnin fired again.

"Call it in," Tinnin said. "Then go back inside and check on them. I'm in pursuit."

Tinnin took two running steps and banged against the outer wall, swearing again as he slid to his seat.

Jake glanced at the retreating truck, resisting the urge to give chase.

"Chief?"

"Go on back there, I said." Tinnin scrambled to retrieve his crutches.

Jake retreated into the building. Lori was inside a closet somewhere with Fortune. He holstered his weapon and retraced his steps, shouting into the radio.

It was early, but there would be at least one unit available, plus anyone on the force who had their radio on. He described the suspects and their yellow pickup. The responses came in from Bear Den and Officer Walter Cooke. Somehow the three men with the most experience on the force were all responding.

Jake reached the nurses' station to find Burl Tsosie standing on shaking legs. He glanced at Jake.

"They gone?"

"Yes. Where's Lori?"

Burl hooked a thumb over his shoulder at the closed utility closet door. "In there."

"Lori?" He rapped on the door. "It's safe. Come out."

The door flew open and Lori dived into his arms, clinging to his chest as she sobbed. His hand came up to cradle her head, and he made shushing sounds to comfort her.

"It's all right now. They're gone. Is she all right?"

"S-s-sleeping," Lori said. She lifted her head enough to turn and glance back at the baby carrier he spied on the floor, tucked tight to the cinder-block wall, beneath a table.

"Good work, Lori. You saved her."

She looked up at him with eyes streaming tears. "They were after her. Weren't they?"

He nodded. "I think so."

"But why?"

From behind them, Burl added his question. "Who were they, anyway?"

Jake helped Lori gather Fortune. Her hands were shaking so badly, he didn't trust her to carry her.

"You okay?" he asked.

She sniffed and nodded.

"They took my tag," said Burl, lifting his empty lanyard.

Jake gave him a once-over. "You hit?"

"Hit? You mean with buckshot? No, I don't think so." Burl went pale and sat heavily in the black swivel chair.

The sound of heels clicking down the hall made Lori flinch. Jake turned to see Betty Mills, eyes wide as she took in the smoke-filled corridor and the results of multiple shotgun blasts.

"What in the name of heaven?" she gasped, her gaze darting from one disaster to the next. "Is everyone okay?"

CHIEF TINNIN PULLED Jack Bear Den away from the FBI investigation of the dam collapse to take the lead at the scene of the attempted abduction. Then they called the Arizona Highway Patrol to help process the scene.

Tinnin's foot had been x-rayed at the clinic, and he'd accepted a new pair of aluminum crutches rather than submit to using a walker.

There was fingerprint powder everywhere, and Betty Mills was apocalyptic at the mess they'd made.

Mills refused to have Fortune taken from the clinic, but Tinnin said he didn't need her permission to take charge of the infant.

"Child Protective Services made the clinic custodian for that baby until temporary placement can be arranged," said Mills.

"And I'm arranging it with Ms. Mott."

Mills did not back down. "She shouldn't be left in charge of that baby," said Mills, pointing at Lori. "She's suspended."

"Well, then, she's got some time on her hands."

Mills glowered.

"Aren't you moving to the trailers up on Turquoise Ridge today?" asked Tinnin.

"I don't understand the rush," said Betty.

"At first we thought the temporary rubble dam would hold," replied Tinnin. "But now, with water continuing to build behind it, the Army Corps says it's not safe. We have to go."

"Everyone?" Lori whispered.

Jake nodded. "It's bad. The water level is still rising. Too much pressure on the rubble. Army Corps stays with police patrol. That's it."

Lori's eyes widened. They might still lose the entire town, despite the brave efforts of FBI agent Sophia Rivas, Wallace Tinnin and Jack Bear Den. And Jake might be on patrol when it happened. The fear struck her deep.

"Koun'nde?" she asked, mentioning the river town to their north.

"Safe for now," Jake said.

Tinnin and Mills still sparred.

"Moving doesn't absolve us of our responsibility of custody of Baby Doe," said Betty.

"Until I know what's going on, I'm assuming that infant was the target of an abduction, and I'm absolving you," said Tinnin.

"We get BOLOs all the time," said Betty. "It could have just been two people who wanted to steal a baby, not specifically *that* baby."

A BOLO was a notice from other area hospitals and meant *Be on the lookout*. Betty Mills had issued one, too, for the tribe's clinic after a confused woman wandered into the women's health clinic asking to see the babies.

"Granted," said Tinnin. "Point being, you've got a mountain of boxes to fill and I've got a registered nurse who is available to help me out."

Mills's gaze drifted to the baby Lori held. "If the tribal council hadn't already taken the only suitable structure large enough to hold a clinic, we would not have to move to those trailers."

Tinnin's brow's lifted. "True enough. Trailers are inbound. So we'll leave you to your packing," said Tinnin, and he turned his back to her, directing his next comments to Jake. "You take Lori and the baby. I've got Burl. Least I don't need crutches to drive."

"I need him," said Mills.

Tinnin glanced over his shoulder. "He's coming in for questioning. Then I'll send him on back."

Jake transported Lori and Fortune to the station. She wanted to walk as the tribe's health clinic and tribal seat were adjacent, but given the circumstances he thought it safer to drive from the clinic, around the block to park in the lot before the tribal headquarters.

She could not explain the relief she felt getting Fortune away from that clinic. How had her workplace become somewhere she no longer felt safe?

It had happened before the intruders, she realized. It had happened the minute she made the connection between the missing girls and the tribe's health care service.

Today was the last day at the police station. They drove through empty streets and unnatural calm. Piñon Forks was abandoned except for emergency personnel and construction teams, and the police force was also moving to trailers in Turquoise Ridge.

Jake pulled them to the spot reserved for handicapped parking because of proximity to the entrance and put his vehicle in Park.

"Walter Cooke will take care of the questioning," Jake said to Lori. "When he's finished, we'll take Fortune to temporary housing."

"Where?" she asked.

"Working on that." He switched off the motor.

He clasped her chin between his thumb and forefinger. He hesitated, casting a quick glance about, and then stared down into her eyes. The heat that flared inside her from that look caught her off guard.

"I'm so glad you're all right," he whispered.

Her heart went from resting to jackhammer as he leaned down and pressed a firm, solid kiss on her lips. Then he straightened, turned and left her.

Her mouth tingled as she watched him climb out of the vehicle. What the heck was happening between them?

Chapter Eight

Tinnin spoke to Jake in his office inside the empty police station. They'd finished with Burl and sent him off. Lori waited with Walter Cooke in the outer office beside Fortune, now perched in her carrier on the wide windowsill.

All the desks, computers and office equipment had been loaded and were on their way to Turquoise Ridge. Only Tinnin's battered wooden desk remained in his office, minus the chair. Tinnin leaned against the surface, facing Jake so he had a view of Walter and Lori.

"Burl didn't see much more of the suspects than we did," said Tinnin, sounding disappointed.

"Any progress on finding the mother?" asked Jake.

"We are looking at local hospitals for women who appear to have recently given birth. Nothing so far." Tinnin's voice echoed on the barren walls. "I agree with your assessment that the clinic appears unsafe, and with the move, it would be better if the infant were elsewhere. I've talked to Dr. Hauser, and he's agreed."

"What does that mean, exactly?"

"It means he doesn't want his clinic treated like a shooting gallery. So Baby Doe is getting an alternate placement."

"Lori and I call her Fortune."

Tinnin's wiry brows lifted. "Do you?"

"Because she was fortunate I found her."

"See, that's not luck. That mother saw you coming."

Jake nodded. "I had the same suspicion."

"I've had Cooke canvassing your neighborhood, asking every family near you if they have any ideas."

The chief referred to Officer Walter Cooke, who had five years on the force and ambitions to earn his detective's shield.

"Any leads?"

"He's working some angles. Meanwhile, I need someone to guard that baby." His gaze rested heavily on Jake.

Jake shifted, growing increasingly uncomfortable under Tinnin's hawkish stare. He rubbed his neck.

"I've never looked after an infant."

"Yet the mother picked you. Left her in your truck."

"Before today, I'd never held a newborn." Except his own, he thought, absorbing the pain that lanced through his heart.

Tinnin offered a rare smile. "Don't worry, Redhorse. Lori will mind the infant. Your job is to keep them both safe while we figure out who's after that baby girl."

A suspicion rose in Jake's mind, and he frowned.

His tough, tired chief of police had a reputation for matchmaking. He'd been the one who assigned Bear Den to work with Sophia Rivas. And he'd been the one to suggest to their shaman that Ray Strong would be the man to watch over Morgan Hooke, whose name had recently changed to Morgan Strong.

Jake was sure that Tinnin knew all about his past with Lori. It would be arrogant to think that Tinnin had done this just to get Lori to speak to him again. But Jake noted a trickling stream of hope moving inside him.

He was still sweating, but now he was sweating like a man who had been given a second chance and didn't want to screw it up.

Five years after the miscarriage, he and Lori were bringing a newborn home from the tribe's health care clinic. It was an eventuality he could not have foreseen.

"For how long?"

"Long as it takes to sort this out."

"What about the move and my other duties?"

"This is the only duty you have to handle until I say otherwise."

Jake nodded, shouldering the responsibility and feeling the weight of two lives settle there.

Tinnin placed a hand on Jake's shoulder. "I've been watching you, son, and I have spoken to our shaman about you. We both want to offer you membership in the Turquoise Guardians."

That was the elite medicine society of their tribe. His brother Ty used to speak about it all the time before their father's arrest. Ty had once set his sights on becoming a member. Jake realized that accepting Tinnin's offer would drive the wedge deeper between him and Ty. He debated his options. To refuse would be an insult.

Like all medicine societies, the Turquoise Guardians' purpose was to strengthen and protect the tribe.

"To protect Lori?"

"Lori's already a member." Tinnin grinned, showing bottom teeth stained with coffee.

That news shocked Jake to speechlessness. Lori had been chosen. That made no sense. How could Lori have been offered membership before him?

"If you accept, you will be welcome at our gatherings, take part in planning meetings and, if you do well, will one day be included as a member of Tribal Thunder."

Tribal Thunder was the warrior sect of the medicine society, and in addition to making detective, it was a lifelong ambition of Jake's.

"What do you say, Redhorse?"

"I'm honored to accept."

"We'll plan a ceremony for the next meeting. Meanwhile, we've arranged for you to take over Wetselline's home on Turquoise Ridge for the time being. He'll take yours. Daniel's place is isolated and has a good view of the valley and approach road. No one is sneaking up on you there."

Except his brother Colt. He could sneak up on anyone. "Colt is up in Turquoise Ridge somewhere."

"Yes." Tinnin looked sad. "I heard. He's not doing too well, is he?"

"No. Ty's the only one who has seen him. He just runs away from the rest of us."

"Still up in that old cabin, the one that Mattson used for hunting the ridge?"

"Yes, sir. He doesn't like to be around people."

"You ask me, you should send Kee up there with a bottle of tranquilizers. He needs some help."

"Kee's tried that. Colt just disappears."

Tinnin popped a piece of nicotine gum into his mouth and started chewing. "Sad state."

A silence dropped between them. Jake shifted, wondering if he should mention his conversation with Ty.

"Sir, my brother Ty has a dog."

The chief lifted his brows and chewed, waiting for Jake to circle around to the point of the subject shift.

"His dog is a very good tracker. He uses her for hunting, but she can track anything that moves, including men."

"Or a woman?" asked Tinnin, zeroing in on Jake's intention.

Jake waited. "I asked him to search my place."

"You already asked him?"

Jake nodded.

Tinnin stopped chewing. Jake knew the chief wouldn't ask Jake's older brother for any favors. Everyone on the force knew Ty had been a member of the Wolf Posse and possibly still was.

"Well, *we* sure haven't found anything." Tinnin

deliberated, then seemed to make up his mind and aimed a finger at Jake. "But as a favor to you. Understand? Not official business. No way."

Tinnin left the rest unsaid. He didn't want to owe a debt to a man with gang ties.

"Yes, sir."

"Doubt he'll find anything. None of your neighbors know of any pregnant white girls running loose. My opinion, the mother drove up here from some suburb and saw your police car, then dropped the baby and took off back out there."

"Out there" was what they all called anywhere off the rez. Folks not from their tribe were also from "out there."

"Maybe," said Jake.

Tinnin blew a long blast of air. "Let's get you and Lori situated. I'd like to be home tonight for supper."

They started for the door, Jake waiting for Tinnin to get his crutches under him before turning the knob.

"Does Lori know she's staying with me at Wetselline's?" he asked, his voice now low and laced with a trepidation he could not name.

Tinnin gave a slow incline of his chin. "Walter was instructed to tell her."

"How'd she take it?" Jake was now looking at Lori, who stared back at him with an expression he could not gauge.

"Guess we'll find out," said Tinnin.

JAKE FOLLOWED AS the chief thumped along on his crutches toward Walter and Lori.

When he reached them, Tinnin explained to Lori the danger of what she was undertaking.

"We're looking for the suspects, but we are also moving this station to Turquoise Ridge, overseeing the safety of the workers at the river and monitoring the water levels."

In other words, Jake thought, his force of seven was strained past the breaking point. They were all operating on little sleep and caffeine. Tinnin glanced at him.

"You up for this assignment, Redhorse?"

"Whatever you need, sir."

"Let's go, then."

Detective Bear Den arrived, pausing to glance around at the empty space, giving a low whistle. Behind him came Jake's eldest brother, Kee.

Jake's stomach pitched. His brother was here for questioning, and from the relaxed expression on his face, Kee did not know what was coming. Jake believed that his brother could not be tied up in the girls' disappearances. But if the clinic was the common thread, then the list of suspects was very small and included his brother and Lori.

Bear Den motioned Kee in and then turned to wait during Tinnin's labored approach. He came to a stop and gave a long sigh.

"How's the ankle?" he asked.

"Hurts like blue blazes."

"He needs a cast," said Kee. "And he's coming to see me later on to get one. We only agreed to the boot when he said he would go slowly."

"When I made that promise, I didn't know I'd be caught in gunfire."

"Let my brother do the running from now on," said Kee.

"See, good advice," said Tinnin.

Bear Den spoke to Tinnin. "I finished with Burl and sent him back to the clinic to help in the move and ran into Dr. Redhorse. Thought you might like to be there when I ask a few questions."

Tinnin nodded and adjusted his crutches, then reversed course back toward his office but was passed by two of the movers, who lifted Tinnin's desk and carried it by them.

"I think the bench is still there," said Tinnin, motioning with his head toward the hallway.

"Nope," said one of the movers as they jostled the desk through the outer door. "Just loaded it."

Tinnin swore.

"Bench out front?" offered Bear Den.

"I need to get back to help at the clinic," Kee said to Tinnin.

"Won't be long," said the chief, and he headed out after the movers.

Kee lingered, smiling at Lori. Jake didn't like the look of that.

"This way, Ms. Mott," said Cooke.

"I'll walk you out," Jake said, but Cooke waved him off.

"I'm to stay with her until Tinnin finishes up. Chief's orders. You've got orders, too, right?"

Jake nodded. Tinnin had told him that.

"You switching cars, right?" asked Cooke.

"Yeah."

Lori gathered Fortune, holding her in her carrier over her crooked arm like an Easter basket. Bear Den held the door.

Kee and Jake trailed behind them, leaving the empty station and heading down the sidewalk to the lot. Jake stayed close to Kee. His oldest brother was no longer unsteady on his feet, but old habits and all.

"Listen, Kee…" What should he say? What was he allowed to say?

Lori lifted the carrier into the back seat of Tinnin's police car. Cooke remained beside the vehicle, scanning for trouble. Jake worried that Cooke would need backup.

Tinnin reached the bench and eased to a seat, jockeying his crutches against his thigh. Bear Den continued on to help Cooke and Lori.

Kee paused, watching Bear Den and Cooke get Fortune strapped in.

"So you're assigned to protect Lori?" asked Kee.

Jake nodded. He was anxious to get the baby and Fortune away from here and the river that was once more a threat. But he felt the tug of responsibility to stay and defend Kee.

"You looking forward to some alone time with Lori?" asked Kee.

"It's an assignment."

"You're an interesting choice, don't you think?"

Jake grimaced. "What is that supposed to mean?"

"You don't get it, do you?" asked Kee.

"Get what?"

"She is not 'that Mott girl' anymore," Kee said in a fair imitation of their mother. "Lori is an educated woman. She's the catch. Get it?"

"But..." His arguments stalled.

Jake closed his mouth.

"At first I thought she was working so hard to prove you wrong or the tribe wrong. Now I wonder... She's not her mother or her sisters. She's like you and me, bad father or no father, and still somehow she's making a good life for herself and everyone around her. That excludes men too stupid to say they're sorry."

"Sorry? Me? For what?"

"Maybe I skipped a class in human genetics, but I believe I still understand conception. Takes two, Jakey. Just like the tango."

"You don't know what happened."

"I think I do," said Kee, his smile broadening.

"You don't."

"Did she force you?"

"Don't be stupid."

"I won't, if you won't."

"I asked her to marry me, didn't I?"

Kee made a sound in his throat. "You did what was expected, like always."

Jake didn't like Kee's tone. It reminded him of Lori calling him her hero with a sarcastic edge that he didn't appreciate.

"What was I supposed to do?"

"Don't know. I do know that you cutting and running made it clear to everyone that you had asked out of obligation. No one blamed you. You came out clean as a new penny. From what I hear, Lori did not fare so well."

They had Fortune situated, and Lori climbed into the rear seat beside the carrier. Cooke and Bear Den glanced back at them, and Bear Den's gaze narrowed.

Jake felt a weight pressing on him. "You think maybe you need a lawyer?"

Kee's brow wrinkled in confusion. "A lawyer? You serious?"

He didn't know about the missing girls all being seen at the clinic, and Jake realized he could not warn him.

He turned to Kee. "Listen, if you feel uncomfortable at any time, you tell them you aren't answering any questions. You're allowed to say that. At any time."

Kee's brows lifted. "You make it sound like I'm under suspicion of a crime. I didn't shoot up the nursery."

Jake pressed a hand to his brother's shoulder. Tin-nin had already refused his request to be there with Kee when they asked him about the missing girls.

"Be careful and remember what I said—'I'm not answering any more questions.' Got it?"

Kee tried for a laugh, but there was real concern in his eyes now.

"Should I be worried, brother?"

Jake nodded.

"Is this about the shooting?"

This time he shook his head. Bear Den was on his

way back to them now. He had returned to the bench but remained standing, eyes on Kee.

"Ready, Doc?" Bear Den asked.

Kee hesitated, then headed for the two men.

Jake followed them with his eyes. Kee cast a worried gaze back at Jake before sitting beside Tinnin. Bear Den closed in, blocking his view. Jake swallowed, but the lump in his throat remained as he prayed that Kee had nothing to do with the disappearances.

Chapter Nine

Jake followed Tinnin's directions, leaving his police unit at the station and switching to one of the cars that his brother Colt had left behind at their parents' place. Bear Den, Tinnin and he all agreed—a yellow truck was very possibly a truck belonging to the Wolf Posse. The attack did not seem like a couple of confused, would-be parents, but rather a targeted hit on the clinic to grab one specific baby. Gang involvement upped the ante considerably.

Jake had asked Ty to help find Baby Fortune's mother and he knew that Ty and Faras Pike, the gang's leader, were tight. Gang involvement worried him because he feared it was possible that Ty might have alerted Faras to Fortune's location and then Faras might have sent his goons. Why they might want this baby was another question.

There were a few yellow trucks on the rez, and it would take some work to run them all down. Bear Den and Cooke would handle that.

Jake knew the owner of one yellow truck. It had belonged to Trey Fields, a known gang member who was currently awaiting trial for the attacks on FBI field agent Sophia Rivas. So who was driving that truck now?

Jake stopped at his place to pack a few things, then headed to Koun'nde and pulled into his mother's driveway.

Duffy Rope spotted him right away, of course, and met him before he reached the front step. Duffy was affable and very good to his mother. But he could talk the ears off an elephant.

"Want something to eat?" Duffy asked.

Jake explained he just wanted to be sure Colt's truck ran.

"Well, Ty comes around and keeps it in shape, hoping, you know, that Colt will drive it again. Ty says Colt doesn't like closed spaces. Me, now, I never considered a car a closed space on account of the windows, I suppose."

Jake made it up the steps and inside to see his mother, with Duffy yapping at him the whole way like a small, friendly dog. He kissed his mom and then felt bad he didn't bring her something. But he remembered that what he usually brought was candy, and she was no longer supposed to eat that.

She rose heavily from her recliner and hugged him. Her color was bad. He glanced to what remained of her left foot. They'd taken the big toe, now leaving her only the three middle ones.

"How are you?" Jake asked.

"Got a sore here on my foot." She extended her

foot to show the bandage. "Cat scratched me and I just don't heal good anymore."

Kee had mentioned the sore to him. He hoped this one healed. His mother eased back into the over-stuffed, sagging chair.

"Have you seen Colt yet?" she asked.

Jake was going to say that he'd tried on more than one occasion, but Colt always disappeared before Jake could find him. Just like the old games of hide-and-seek. No one could find Colt unless he wanted to be found.

"Not yet."

"Well, I need to see that boy with my own eyes. You tell him so."

"Yes, Mama."

"Abbie is worried about him. And she needs to see her brothers. Lord knows she don't listen to me."

Abbie was his sister, just thirteen. She was a good kid, but recently she vacillated between caring for and fighting with her mother. Her teen years had begun, and as her body changed, so did her disposition. Jake didn't like to think of her becoming a woman, though since her sunrise ceremony, she was a woman in the eyes of this tribe and a full member of the Turquoise Canyon Apache.

"She's got a boyfriend," said his mother.

"What? Who?"

"Donny Hosie. She talks on that phone you got her until after midnight."

Better than being out with him until then, Jake

thought. He made a mental note to find Donny and have a talk with him.

"What about Kee? You see him, don't you?" she asked.

"Yes, just today," said Jake.

"He's so busy with the clinic move and then at the Darabee hospital. I thought when he finished his residency he would have more free time. Maybe he does, but he sure don't come round here, and I'm giving up hope he'll ever find a wife."

Kee had been the first one to get off the rez, and he only came back to work at the clinic. He had the most memories of their dad and said there was a time when he had been a father to them. Jake couldn't recall that far back. As far as Jake was concerned, Kee and Ty were more father than his real one.

"I'll tell him you want him to stop by."

"I make him feel guilty, is what, on account of the fact that he can't fix me."

"Mama, I need the keys to Colt's car."

"Why?"

"Undercover work."

"Really?" Her face brightened. "Is that why you're not in uniform?"

He grinned and nodded.

His mother clapped her hands. She loved watching all the police procedural television shows and could not understand why it took so long to catch a criminal in real life when the detectives in nearly every show had the bad guys caught, tried and sentenced in under an hour, including commercial breaks.

He nodded. "Yes, ma'am."

"You aren't even a detective yet."

"It's a protective detail."

The sparkle went out of her eyes. "This doesn't have to do with that woman, does it?"

His stomach dropped. His mother rarely left the house, but her information network rivaled the network news stations. Duffy was one of her sources. Jake cast him a look and he shrugged.

"Mama…"

"Lori Mott. I heard you were at the station with her."

Obviously she had not yet heard about the attack at the clinic.

"Still trying to snare you like a rabbit, is what."

Jake wondered what she would think if she knew Kee had tried to date her.

"It's complicated, Mama."

"No, Jakey. It's not. She's got a reputation."

Jake refrained from reminding her that her son Ty was a known associate of the Wolf Posse. You never left a gang, not without leaving the rez, so that meant Ty was still on the opposite side.

His mother persisted. "Those Mott gals are all alike, and don't even get me started on her mother. She can't even settle on one man."

Kee's words seemed to reverberate in his head. Jake cared about Lori, but there was a time when he had been relieved that he didn't have to marry "one of the Mott girls." Lori's actions said his mother had been wrong and was wrong now.

"She's not like that," Jake said, his voice low.

"She is exactly like that."

"Mom, I love you, but if you keep up with this, you won't see me any more than you see Kee or Colt."

The look of shock lifted his mother's thinning brows, and she stammered. Jake had always done what he thought would make his mother proud, and except for one mistake, he had done that. That one mistake he had allowed his mother to pin firmly elsewhere. Now, seeing this from a different angle, he had doubts, including whether whatever he did would ever be enough.

Kee said he should apologize to Lori.

"I just want what's best for you, Jakey."

Jake retrieved the keys from the fishbowl that included matches and loose change. "What if she's best for me, Mom?"

His mother's jaw dropped. When she recovered and found her words, it was the same old refrain. "Sh-she tried to trap you."

"Mama, we had sex. Teenagers do that and we didn't use protection. *I* didn't use it. It was *my* fault, because I convinced her to have sex, and *not* the other way around. Understand?"

She blinked at him in stunned silence.

"I'm still on duty. I have to go."

He kissed her offered cheek. She gripped his hand, tethering him.

"Dinner next Sunday?"

"Working."

She turned to Duffy. "Working. He's working.

Kee's working. Ty's working, and my baby is living up in the woods like one of our ancestors."

"Give him some time, Mama."

"Ty won't even tell me what happened to him. I opened his mail. You can go on and arrest me. He was discharged with psychiatric issues. Did you know that?"

He did.

"You know where he went when he come home? Not here to his family. No, he went to Kacey Doka's house, but she'd already run off. Ty said Colt took that real hard."

The only female his mother liked less than Lori was Kacey Doka. She'd once championed the girl, who had lived with them for several months. But that was before Colt took an interest in her. Now his mother blamed Colt's current problems on Kacey's disappearance, though Colt's discharge and Kacey going missing seemed unrelated. Jake wondered if it was possible that his mother would dislike any woman who had the audacity to date one of her boys.

Jake drew his hand free.

"She didn't run off. She's missing, Mama. Her family hasn't heard from her."

"Why would they, way they treated her? She lived in this house more than at home until she up and left without even a word of goodbye. I'm just furious over it. Duffy, bring me some soda."

Jake never understood why his mother hated Lori Mott for her family and felt sorry for Kacey Doka over hers.

"All we have is diet."

"Don't give me that. I know what you have in that refrigerator."

"Bye, Mama."

"You be careful, Jakey."

And then he was back out in the cool night. He took a moment to breathe the crisp air. His mother had been in a bad marriage. It was one of the reasons she was choosy about the women her sons dated.

Jake had been happy when his father had been taken away by Wallace Tinnin, the man he always wished had been his father. That might have been the day that he decided to become a police officer. He wanted to take away men who hurt women and their own kids.

He slipped behind the wheel of the 1957 Chevy pickup that had been rusting out in a pasture before Ty claimed it. His brother had traded the owner free tune-ups on his truck for life. Ty had said that he was reckless and the cattleman old, so it would be a good deal one way or the other. Then he had proceeded to change the old red rust bucket into a gleaming thing of beauty.

Jake never cared for the colors until he'd learned why Ty had picked them. His choice was purely because neither mint nor maroon was found in any gang's colors. He did not want his baby brother caught in Wolf Posse territory in a red truck, the color of their rival gang, or flashing gang colors. Ty meant to beat Colt senseless if he ever thought about joining a gang. It was the sort of tough love that they

never received from their father. Jake had a feeling
Ty would have turned out differently if someone had
given him a mint-green truck.

The Chevy also had maroon detail lines that became a group of charging horses on the front fenders.
Ty's work, of course—colts on a Chevy and a play
on Colton's nickname. Ty had become quite an artist.
He had chosen the peculiar color palette for one other
reason: it was distinctive enough to identify Colt immediately as Ty's brother, and therefore off-limits to
any in the Wolf Posse.

Jake had never needed Ty's protection because
Jake gained respect from his popularity in school
and his prowess on the basketball court. Now he had
the protection of the law, which he enforced, and the
family of his fellow officers.

Had his boss, Chief Tinnin, suggested Colt's truck
because it was known by the Wolf Posse? And also
because it was known that the only ones who ever
drove it were Colt and Ty? This truck was the prover-
bial wolf in sheep's clothing. Or in this case, a sheep
in wolf's clothing.

Ty's hair was shoulder length and hung shaggy
around his face. But their faces were similar enough
to fool a casual observer. He thought Tinnin knew
that when he'd suggested this.

He sure hoped so.

Halfway to the station, he pulled over and rested
his hands on the wheel before pressing his forehead
to the backs of them. Bear Den had told him they
had failed to locate the baby's mother. They were

processing evidence and speaking to neighbors, but the missing girls and the evacuation resulting from the dam failure were top priorities. They had no matches on the prints taken from the infant's foot and palm. In other words, no one seemed to be missing a baby. In fact, no newborns were missing this month anywhere in the country.

So they were looking at a crime. A new mother who had birthed her baby and left it for him to find or not. He couldn't understand it. Even when he'd been a frightened kid of sixteen with a basketball scholarship and a career chosen, he never thought of giving away his flesh and blood. He'd been ready to defy his mother's wishes, stop everything, marry Lori and raise their child. But when Lori lost their baby, he'd been off the hook, and he'd taken no time to put the entire incident behind him.

He'd wanted to be a good husband and father, if a young one. But he'd never gotten the chance to be either. Funny how the years never made that tug in his chest go away. He longed to try again with Lori and this baby. But first he had to get Lori to stop being so dang mad at him about what had happened between them. Kee had given him a suggestion on where to start. An apology.

Trouble was, he wasn't sure he deserved her forgiveness.

Chapter Ten

Lori sat in the back seat of the chief's SUV beside Fortune in the infant car seat. Police chief Tinnin drove his personal vehicle, taking her far out toward Darabee in a roundabout route that would involve a vehicle switch and several of the officers, to be certain they were not followed.

She had everything she needed to take care of a newborn for several days, along with some personal items, thanks to the help of Carol Dorset, the dispatcher for tribal police, who had gone to Lori's home with the key Lori provided. She'd left it up to Carol as to what she might need.

She should be worrying about whoever had tried to snatch Fortune, but instead she was thinking about Jake and the kiss he'd given her in the car outside the station. But the kiss didn't bother her nearly as much as that little thing he'd done before kissing her. It had barely registered at the time, but he'd paused and glanced around to be certain they were alone. Did he want privacy, or did he want to be sure nobody saw him kissing her?

The shame welled, familiar and bitter.

Soon she would be holed up in a stranger's home with the man she had once planned to marry.

She thought she'd set up barriers between them so strong he'd never get through. But just like the dam above their rez, her barriers were not impenetrable. She knew this because she felt them cracking under the strain of his proximity.

His kiss told her that he still had feelings for her. But her experience told her that for whatever reason, she wasn't good enough to marry the golden boy of the Redhorse family. So, fine, she didn't need him, but what she would not do was sneak around with him. He might succeed in going out with her if he showed some contrition and shouldered his share of the blame for their pregnancy, but she was not coming and going by the back door ever again.

They pulled into the parking garage that adjoined the larger regional hospital in Darabee. She glimpsed the lights from the helicopter pad as they made the turn. One of their own tribe members, Kurt Bear Den, worked there as a paramedic. Tinnin wound his way up to the third level and pulled into the handicapped spot before the elevators, then parked facing out. Jack Bear Den waited. He approached the driver's side window and spoke to Tinnin.

There had been no traffic in the last half hour on this level. A few moments later, she spied a familiar mint-green pickup, Jake's brother Ty behind the wheel. The truck stopped before them, and she blinked as she realized that she'd been wrong. The man exiting the truck was not Ty but Jake, dressed in jeans and a black T-shirt that advertised APTN, Aboriginal Peoples Television Network. The center logo showed a television with antennae drawn like eagle feathers. It was exactly the sort of thing Ty would wear—and Jake would not.

"All set," he said to Wallace.

"Good."

He could talk around her now, but in a few minutes they'd be alone in that mint-green Chevy truck—and then what?

Jake moved the three bags from the seat beside her to the truck bed, and she carefully unfastened the car seat, then transferred it and baby Fortune to the passenger's side of the truck. The infant really should be in the back seat, but there was none. No airbags, either, she supposed. Didn't the men think of that when they'd chosen this vehicle?

It was only then that she recognized this meant she would have to sit in the center of the truck, just like the night in Jake's truck when they had been young and in love and she had believed that nothing in the world could keep them apart.

THEY DROVE IN darkness through Piñon Forks and Koun'nde to the higher elevations well past any potential flood area. He had been given temporary use of Daniel Wetselline's home, since he was on duty tonight and his house would be empty. He pulled into the unfamiliar drive late in the evening and used the borrowed key to get them inside.

Lori carried Fortune into the darkened entrance, and Jake flipped on the light. Jake had a look around, and Lori took Fortune into the master bedroom to get them both ready for bed. She was feeding Fortune when Jake came in to check on them.

"You going to sleep in here?" He indicated the queen bed by lifting his chin.

She nodded. Fortune's eyes drooped and she sucked with less intensity as sleep dragged at her.

"Hungry?" he asked Lori.

"Thirsty."

"I'll meet you out in the kitchen."

Lori got Fortune washed up and changed. She walked her about the room as she had done with many fussy babies, but this felt different. She was in a home, to begin with. But that wasn't it.

She admitted what was inside her heart to Fortune in the quiet of the bedroom. "I'm not going to want to give you up, boo."

Fortune gurgled and her eyes closed. Lori turned to breathe in the sweet scent of the infant and brush her lips over the soft fuzz on her head. Then she lay Fortune down in her bassinet, hoping the infant would sleep a few hours before waking again.

Lori took a deep breath and smoothed her hair, gathering herself to meet Jake in the kitchen.

He greeted her with a smile and offered her cereal with milk and a large glass of sweet tea. Jake refilled his bowl and joined her at the table. She finished the offering and had a second cup of tea.

"Want to watch some television?" he asked.

"What time is it?"

He checked his wristwatch. "Nearly midnight."

"I think I'll turn in. See if I can get a few hours of sleep before she wakes up again," said Lori.

"I can see to her. I'm used to waking up in the night. I'm on call for accidents and such, and I'm a light sleeper."

"We'll see." She sent him a smile, and he returned it. They stood in unison, then cleared the dishes to the sink. He moved closer and stopped just inside her personal space.

She tucked her arms about her, wishing she had the courage to wrap them around Jake.

"Thanks for helping me take care of her, Lori."

"Of course." She rocked from heel to toe, delaying their parting. They were completely alone now, and she found her will to resist Jake Redhorse crumbling.

She tented her brows and waited for him to make the first move. He didn't.

"Good night, Lori."

She dropped her gaze, letting the disappointment seep through her. He'd kissed her in front of the station. Why not now?

He glanced from her to the couch, all made up and waiting, and she had her answer. Jake had already calculated what would happen next. Stealing a kiss was one thing. Being alone with her for an entire night was quite another. Her lust died at this confirmation that Jake, while attracted to her, was not interested in a relationship with her.

The temptation that neither one of them had ever had

any control over was leaping between them again. Just like high school. Only now Lori was older and wiser.

Well, older anyway.

"You're not taking the other bedroom?" she asked.

"It's an office. No bed."

"Ah. Well, good night, Jake."

He stepped in and kissed her on the top of her head, as if she were both six and his sister. She cast her eyes down but did not close them, and so she saw the evidence of his arousal, clearly visible and jutting from his loose sweats. Her desire was more secret but still there in the aching wetness and the rapid draw of breath. He pushed her toward the hallway.

She left and only paused to glance back at him once before heading into Daniel Wetselline's bedroom to check on Fortune. The infant slept peacefully, so she headed to bed.

The sheets were cold as she slipped in between them and dragged up the covers. She imagined Jake out in the living room, nearly naked, fully aroused. The lure of him dangled before her, and she struggled to resist the urge to go to him. She succeeded only when she thought of him checking that the coast was clear before kissing her.

They were alone now and no one was looking, but he still saw her and their baby as a mistake.

THE SQUAWK OF an infant woke her and she thought for a moment that she had dozed off at work, until she found herself stretched out in an unfamiliar bed. She groped in the dark to find the bedside table and her phone, which illuminated at her touch to tell her it was 3:21 a.m. on Monday morning.

She rose as her thoughts and memories fused to bring back where she was and why she was here. This was the guest bedroom in the home of tribal police officer Daniel Wetselline. She was here with Fortune, who slept in her bassinet just across the room. The baby girl cried in her tiny, quavering voice, but by the time Lori rose, she spotted a familiar shadow appear in the doorway and move to Fortune. Jake lifted her and rested her against his broad bare chest. He stood in only a pair of low-slung cotton sweatpants, his shirt abandoned for sleep. Fortune continued to wail as Lori flicked on the bedside lamp. Her skin was so pink against the smooth brown of Jake's neck and shoulder. One big hand cupped her bottom, and the other her head and neck. The baby's cheek was pressed to his skin.

"I'll get her formula," said Lori, changing course toward the kitchen.

Jake nodded. "I'll change her and be right out."

"You change diapers? Since when?" She cast him a smile over her shoulder.

"I watched some infant care videos on my phone," he said.

Lori motioned Jake to go ahead.

Jake lifted the baby, speaking in a low, comforting voice. Something twisted inside her as she watched him, glimpsing the life they might have had.

This was like a dream, Lori thought. She felt as if she were staring at the scene she had pictured so often: Jake with their baby girl in the home they never made.

She stepped closer. His back was to her, but she could see he held Fortune in his arms and was telling her what a beautiful girl she was. The infant made little cooing sounds as Jake set her on the dresser, now draped in a padded portable changing mat. He made short work of the bundling and got right to work with a gentle manner she rarely saw. Her insides were turning to mush, and she had to force herself not to reach out to him. He had the fresh diaper out and was studying it. He turned, casting her a smile that nearly melted her into a puddle. Those white teeth and that handsome face—he'd only gotten better-looking as he'd grown. His jaw and brow were more prominent, and the dark stubble on his cheeks left no doubt that this was now a man.

He waved the diaper. "Is this the front?"

She nodded and stepped forward, taking the diaper.

"It's so small," he said.

She set the diaper in place, finding Fortune clean and dry. The soiled diaper lay in a tight ball beside her onesie.

"Yes. Newborn size." Lori showed him how to fasten the diaper and then let him wrap Fortune back in her bundling. She lay still, with big blue eyes staring up at them. What must she think, looking at them standing over her?

They worked like new parents, but this was not their child. That time had never come to be. But why, then, were they here now? It seemed as if the universe had sent them back to repeat a turn that they had missed.

"Strange, isn't it?" she asked.

His smile seemed one of complete contentment. "Hmm?"

"Being here like this."

"Yeah." He wrapped Fortune in a soft cotton blanket, lifted her to his shoulder and turned to speak to the baby. "You hungry, my girl?"

Only, she wasn't his. Could he make her so?

Lori followed Jake to the kitchen. He rocked the baby as she heated the formula, checking the temperature because of the unfamiliar microwave. Fortune's sounds were becoming more demanding when she offered him the bottle.

"Me?" he asked.

"Of course."

He carried Fortune to the living room and the large, lopsided recliner. Then he sat and lifted the bottle to the baby's lips. Fortune latched on and Lori again felt her breasts tighten. She crossed her arms over her chest and watched Jake with the baby. He had a marvelous dumb grin on his face, as if hypnotized by the infant as she sucked. He glanced up and cast her a look of amazement.

"She's really hungry."

Lori smiled past the lump in her throat. Jake would have made a wonderful father. They might have had another child already, possibly two or three. And he'd be working at whatever job he could find, and she'd still be a cashier at the grocery store. They'd be broke, surviving until the yearly allotment like most folks here. That was when livestock was purchased and roofs repaired.

She pictured that life, gone now. And she compared it to what she had, material things, an education and a career she loved.

Her heart gave her no doubts—she wanted what she had missed. Worse still, she wanted a family with this man, which was terrible trouble because Jake still saw her as the girl she had been, or perhaps the one she had been cast as by others. If he wanted her, he would not have dropped her to handle her grief alone after their child had died. Oh, he had attended the funeral and done everything else that was expected of him. And then he had slipped back into his life, shedding her like a snake sheds its skin.

Trying again with Jake was just stupid. She judged the girth of his shoulders and the flexing biceps that wrapped around the infant. She didn't want a man like this, who could leave her behind so very easily. But her body wanted him. The longing in the pit of her stomach was growing by the hour. Was it best to address the desire or ignore it?

Sex and a relationship were not synonymous. She knew that—now that she was older. But somehow she believed that sleeping with Jake would be like pulling at a loose thread, and her carefully woven control would unravel. The first time she had fallen for him, she had not understood the risk she took or the pain that would follow his leaving. But if she let him in her heart again, she would deserve what she got. She was wiser now. Wasn't she?

She took a step closer. Could she keep this merely physical? Her heart clenched. Lori gave in, resigning herself. His appeal was too strong. She could not resist touching him again.

"You do that so well," she said.

He glanced at Lori and smiled but then returned his attention to Fortune. She'd seen that blissful look of total happiness before, but usually in the faces of young parents at the clinic. Jake, she realized, was bonding with that baby. And what would happen when they took her away from him?

It seemed cruel of the universe to take two infants from them. But that was what would happen. Fortune would stay in the tribe's clinic until the police finished their investigation. If no relatives could be found, then the infant would be situated in a temporary home and later placed for adoption. Lori had seen it before. They had a list of families willing to shelter newborns until permanent arrangements could be made within the tribe. But this was not an Apache baby. If looks were any judge, this one had none of the characteristics of the Tonto people. The Tonto Apache, their people, shared their roots with the Mountain Apache, but not their language. Of course, Fortune could have some trace of indigenous blood, but not the quarter required to claim status as a Turquoise Canyon Apache member. The only way around that rule was if she were adopted by one or more members of the tribe. Adoptive children were given full rights in their tribe. Always had been.

"Should we give her another bottle?" he asked as the baby drained the first.

"No. Too much food will upset her stomach. Lift her up and rub her back."

Jake did so and Fortune burped. Jake laughed. The sound was infectious, and she laughed, as well. He brought the newborn down to rock in his arms. She stared up at him with a tiny wrinkle in her forehead.

He chuckled. "She doesn't know what to make of me."

Jake's hair was loose around his shoulders now. His smile transformed him—he looked so happy it made her heart ache again. She held her smile as he glanced up at her.

"Isn't she a beauty?"

She nodded. "All babies are beautiful."

"How could someone just give her away?"

"Lots of reasons."

He looked back at Fortune. "I'd never give her away."

Uh-oh, she thought. This was trouble, because as far as she knew, the tribe had never given a baby to a single man. Jake's chances of getting even temporary custody were slim. They had only sent him here with her as protection. Their tribe's traditions had changed in many ways, but not so much that they were inclined to let a single man raise a baby who was not his by birth.

"Jake?" she said.

"She's getting sleepy." Jake began to speak to Fortune in Tonto Apache. He spoke well, she realized, but Jake had always been a good student. He told Fortune of their people, as if this infant was one of them or soon would be.

"You know it's only temporary, right?" she asked.

"What?" he asked, still gazing down at Fortune.

"All this. The house, the family, that little baby. It's not real. She'll be placed in a foster home with a woman and hopefully a family. She won't be placed with you."

Now he looked at her, his brows descending, and she saw something she had never seen before—the protective glare of a parent facing a threat to his child.

"I found her," he said. "I'm keeping her."

Lori pressed her lips together and counted to ten. Then she spoke.

"You are not the only one in love with that baby girl."

"You fixing to challenge me for custody?"

That was one way of playing it. Why did he always think she was after something?

"I'm not challenging you. I'm not trying to trap you. But the parents have rights."

"Her mother left her with me."

"That's not the same as custody."

"I know that."

"Do you?"

"Lori, one thing I know is the law."

"Fine." She blew out a breath and let her gaze drift, then she brought it back to him. "I just want what is best for her."

"And you're saying that I'm not what's best?"

"Parents who want her. Two of them. A home, Jake. That's what's best."

Chapter Eleven

Jake showered, shaved and dressed in his uniform after Fortune's second feeding a little after six o'clock in the morning. When he reached the kitchen to make coffee, he found the pot nearly full. He heard Lori make her way to the bathroom. What in the wide world was he going to do? He wanted Fortune and he wanted Lori. Regrettably, he had no idea how to convince Lori to stay or the tribe to give him temporary custody of Fortune. But he feared Lori was thinking of when she could get rid of him.

Lori had described how things were, the rational, practical explanation. Fortune needed two parents, and no matter how he played it in his mind, he couldn't figure how he'd work and care for a newborn. But Jake was determined to figure out a way to make this happen. Maybe they could have joint temporary custody, or he could have Lori stay with Fortune at night and he could have her during the day. The guys on the force would be delighted to have him take nights.

"Yeah, that will work," he muttered and poured a

cup of coffee. That first swallow was always necessary. The second was a pleasure. He stood at the sink. The dirty dishes there showed she'd already had some coffee, likely while he was in the shower. Avoiding him. Well, that was just great.

He looked at nothing in particular as he tried to determine what to do next. Toast, he decided and began preparations.

Lori didn't seem to want this baby. Well, he'd found that baby girl and he was keeping her, one way or another. He wanted Lori, too, but in a lustful way that he was not sure translated to the sort of enduring partnership needed to raise a child. And she clearly held a grudge against him, which he might deserve. He'd almost kissed her again this morning, when they were changing Fortune. He knew this was more than just scratching an itch or taking a stroll down memory lane. The flame still burned, all right—scorched, in fact. Had it really been as good as he remembered?

"Better," he said and drained the remains of his coffee and then retrieved his toast. He slathered it with peanut butter, then ate standing up at the sink as he drained a second cup of coffee. This was how he usually ate—alone, standing up in his kitchen. And he hated it.

He wanted a family. He wanted Lori, despite what everyone thought of them or what had happened. Did anyone but his mother really care anymore? Lori still cared. That was certain.

The sound of something striking the glass above the sink made him jump. His gaze flicked to the backyard. Just then the pebbles struck the window again, and he spotted Ty standing with Hemi in the yard beside the empty, leaning birdbath.

Hopefully, Ty had some information from his attempt at tracking Fortune's mother and he wasn't there about another problem relating to their brother Colt.

Jake went to the back door. His gaze flicked to Colt's truck, the one Ty had customized for his baby brother. The one Jake had borrowed without permission. He was sure Ty would have something to say about that.

Ty had purchased an old truck for Kee and somehow kept the heap running all through med school but had never offered a vehicle to Jake, and it rankled him more than he cared to admit.

Up until yesterday, he and Ty hadn't really talked much.

Jake sighed. Ty wouldn't talk to him. Kee avoided coming home, except to check on their mother's diabetes, and seemed to be setting up a whole new life in Darabee near the hospital with a group of professional friends Jake had never met. Abbie had a boyfriend, which opened all kinds of terrifying possibilities. And Colt, well, he was here but just gone.

Jake cleared the door and descended to the yard. The air held a morning chill, and the sky had turned a soft peach in preparation for sunrise.

"I didn't hear you pull up," said Jake.

"Because I didn't. I parked in the woods a ways back."

Jake resented that Ty avoided ever being seen with him. It hurt to know that his brother so disapproved of him. Was that why Ty had been so insistent that Jake never join the gang? He'd actually burned those bridges early by making sure that Jake was unwelcome there. He had made it clear that the gang was *his* family. Jake could go find his own. And he had, in the tribal police department. Now those guys were more like brothers to him than either Kee or Ty. When had that happened?

"Hemi got a hit. Tracked the mother to a house."

Everyone, including Jake, assumed the mother had driven in and dropped the baby, then left. But no one could explain to him how the mother had known that Jake was a tribal police officer.

"She didn't come in a car?"

"Seems not. Whoever she is, she's staying with a neighbor of yours—or was, anyway."

"Which one?"

"The Colelay family."

"Colelay?" Jake puzzled over that. He knew this particular family, as he had been there on more than one occasion for domestic disputes. There had even been consideration of removing the children from Mrs. Colelay's custody. She was an addict and alcoholic and spent more on her habits than on her children's maintenance. She had no husband but a series of relationships, and at Jake's last count she had seven children by various fathers.

"You think Irma Colelay had that child?" asked Jake.

"How do I know? You asked me to track the mother and I tracked her. She left your house and went to the line of pines. She was there a while, according to Hemi. She left and went to the Colelay house, and then she came back by the back door and stood near the road in the pines again." Ty scratched the thick scruff around the neck of his dog.

Jake thanked Ty for the information. Ty straightened and regarded Jake in silence for a moment.

"I see you have Colt's truck."

"Yeah."

"You should put it back."

"That right?" asked Jake. He knew Ty would not be happy that he was driving Colt's truck, but his approach was odd. Cryptic, even.

"Sooner is better."

"Why is that?"

Ty glanced toward the woods, as if anxious to be gone. "Just that there have been inquiries. I'm not sure they believe that I don't know where you are."

Jake didn't have to ask who *they* might be. They all believed that someone in the Wolf Posse had made the attack on the clinic yesterday based on the truck colors, and that the pair had been targeting Fortune, just as he feared.

"Is it safe here?" asked Jake, a knot twisting his gut.

"For now. But if I were looking, I'd try the home of every police officer on your tiny force." He started away and then paused. "Maybe they'll go alphabetically and you'll be in luck. Me, I'd start with the junior officers and work up. Danny only has a year on you, right?"

The knot tightened.

"Don't bring her home to Mama."

Jake snorted. "That's the last place I'd bring her. Mom hates Lori."

Ty's stare was accusing. "Well, she had to blame someone and that wouldn't be you. But that's not why. They're watching our house."

"Why do they want this baby?"

He shrugged. If he knew, he wasn't talking. Jake gripped his utility belt as he tried and failed to tamp down the rising anger.

What if they were also targeting Fortune's mother? And now he had brought Ty right in the middle of this.

"Ty, maybe this was a bad idea."

Ty's expression turned stormy. "You afraid I'll give you up?"

"No. I'm afraid you'll reveal the mother's location." His brother gave him a long look. Jake thought he saw disappointment in his brother's eyes.

"I don't have time for this."

"What's going on? How would Mrs. Colelay give birth to a blond baby, and why would she abandon it?"

"You're the police officer. You figure it out."

Before he could stop himself, he lashed out. "Too busy souping up another car for your posse?"

Ty scowled at him and Jake lowered his chin, almost hoping for a fight. They needed to clear the air. Maybe a fistfight was just the ticket.

But Ty changed the subject and took the wind from Jake's sails.

"I've been busy with Colt. He lets me see him sometimes. I talk to him. I think he's listening."

Jake's anger vanished like mist. Of course Ty was looking after Colt, just like always.

"I'm sorry. I should have known."

Ty snorted and turned. His enormous dog rose and stretched, then followed her master toward the tree line, casting one glance back at Jake before the two of them reached the pine forest behind the house.

Jake thought about Mrs. Colelay and her kids. How many daughters did she have, and what were their ages?

"Any chance you and Hemi would come with me to see my neighbors?" called Jake.

Ty did not pause as he and his dog stepped into the tree line and disappeared.

JAKE OPENED THE kitchen door to the sound of water running. He found Lori at the sink, running water into an oddly shaped plastic thing that kept the baby in an inclined position.

"That's wonderful," he said, watching the proceedings. He would love to know how to bathe an infant.

Lori used only a small amount of warm water in the sink. Fortune seemed delighted with the water, kicking and splashing her arms in an uncoordinated motion that Jake found completely adorable.

He laughed. Soon Lori was laughing as well, and his hand was circling her waist. He wanted to keep them here, right here in this spot forever, with the joy bubbling in his heart and the baby gurgling and Lori smiling as if none of the rest had ever happened.

Was he ready for that kind of happiness? More important, was Lori willing to let him back into her life?

She was lifting the dripping, wiggling baby with an expertise he found so enviable. Would he ever have the chance to be so adept at holding a baby? He longed for that experience, wanted it deep in the marrow of his bones.

But Ty's warning intruded. They had to go. But where?

The soft hand towel went around the baby's naked backside, and Fortune went to Lori's shoulder. Fortune waved her hand and managed to clasp hold of a strand of Lori's black hair.

He stepped up behind Lori, and she turned Fortune to look at him. The little infant stared up, eyes widening, and then she gave him her first official smile.

"Oh, do you see that?" said Lori. "She likes you."

That was a very good thing, because that baby already had his heart.

A golden haze circled around Jake that had little to do with the changing leaves or the autumn sunlight.

Kee's words came to him. He should apologize. He'd pretended he didn't understand, but he did. The minute they'd been freed of the pressure of marriage and the notoriety of their pregnancy, he had wanted no more of her. The only thing he had wanted was more distance. Yet when he needed her, she had come.

He couldn't figure out how to explain why he hadn't called or visited her again after they had buried their child. Why he had not spoken up when other people blamed Lori for the entire misstep. His girlfriend hadn't dumped him. He wasn't on the rebound. He'd left Alice for Lori, and he'd never expected to go so fast. But something had happened—had always happened when he was with Lori and no one else. She was *the woman* for him. His heart knew it, even if his mind hadn't.

Alice had told everyone that Lori had cut in behind her back. It wasn't true. Jake should have said so, instead of pretending he didn't know what was happening.

But he was afraid that if he tried to explain his tangled-up emotions now, he'd just drive her off. He understood. Lori had agreed to come here despite him, not because of him.

But now that she was here, something was happening between them again. She felt it, too, didn't she?

"Lori?" he said, fearing that he was ruining the moment even as he opened his mouth, but wanting so much more.

"Hmm?" she said, smiling down at Fortune.

"I'm so glad you're here."

And then she was smiling at him, too.

He held Fortune while she prepared a bottle. She came back to him with a small warm bottle in one hand and a welcoming smile on her lips. Before he could remember that she was here for the baby and he for their protection, he reached out and laced his fingers through her hair.

She hesitated as her gaze flashed to his, reading his intention in his eyes, and then she stepped toward him, lifting her chin and parting her full lips. Acceptance, he realized.

He swooped, taking her mouth in a kiss that he had intended to be sweet and gentle. Instead, the lustful prelude gave way to a second and a third. These were the kind of kisses that were shared between lovers long parted, between souls that yearned for the connection of one body to another. He drank her in, tasting the salty sweetness of her mouth. Lori gave a sound of need deep in her throat as their tongues slid back and forth. His hand moved from her hair and ran up and down her back. She stepped forward, pressing against him. She turned, angling so her hip met the center of him, and she rubbed against his arousal. His hand went under her soft T-shirt.

Fortune made a sound that he had come to recognize preceded her crying, a sort of staccato series of chirps, as if to remind them both that she had not yet been fed.

Lori broke away, and he let her go. His timing sucked. For a moment they both just stared at each other in a mix of wonder and horror.

"Overdue, I'm afraid," he said.

"But still an incredibly bad idea."

"I don't think so."

She lifted her brows, casting him a look of disbelief.

"Jake Redhorse, we have had no more than polite conversation since I got back on the rez, and now, today, you kiss me like…like…like that?"

"I tried to talk to you, Lori. You weren't having it."

"You don't get a pass, Jake. Before this happened, the last time we had a conversation that lasted more than a minute, it was at the grave of our daughter."

That was true.

"You wouldn't talk with me, Lori. Not about anything that mattered."

"Because I still have some pride left, Jake."

What did that even mean?

She reached for Fortune, plucked her from his arms and held her to receive her breakfast. Fortune smacked her lips in anticipation. Then Lori held Fortune as she sucked on the bottle.

"So you're saying we need to talk first."

"First?" Her gaze flicked to the ceiling and held there, as if she were counting to ten. Then she met his gaze. "We have some things to work through. No matter how well we fit or how much I'm tempted to, I know you, and you are not staying around after we sleep together."

"That's not true."

"No? Then let's go visit your mother. Tell her we're a couple."

Now his gaze flicked away, resting on the floor.

She made a sound in her throat.

"Is that what you want, Lori? To be a couple?"

"I don't know, Jake. But I sure know what I don't want. I don't want to be your dirty little secret. And I don't want you to hurt me again."

"I never meant to."

"You knew what Alice was saying about me. You had to know what everyone was saying."

He did. "I didn't encourage them, though."

The sound she made seemed one of exasperation, landing somewhere between a humph and a growl. "You didn't stand up to them, Jake. You didn't tell them that you were the one who broke up with Alice. That we were a couple, and *we* had sex. You left me out there. Do you know what her friends called me?"

He didn't. But he did remember what Alice had asked him. At the time, it seemed a small thing. Now he realized he'd loaded the shotgun that Alice had used to fire at Lori.

"She said it would help her save face if I said she dumped me," said Jake.

Lori's voice went low and dangerous. "So you were worried about *her* feelings? Protecting *her* from gossip?"

"I didn't think…"

"That's for sure." She spun, presenting him with her back.

"It was just words."

Lori rounded on him. "Words? They called me a slut. A little tramp, and worse. Every day until I graduated. Two years of being the girl who dared to have sex with you. And you never came back to me. Never proved to them that I didn't trick you or seduce you."

"You wouldn't speak to me, Lori."

"Do you blame me?"

Fortune finished draining the bottle. Lori lifted the infant to her shoulder and walked away. He didn't know what to say to Lori because she was right. He had distanced himself from her at her request. He had no idea Alice's little groupies had been so cruel. But that was also his fault. He shouldn't have let Lori push him away, and now that he knew why she had done so, he felt even worse.

"I should have stopped them. I should have done

something. I didn't know how bad it was for you. I—I…" There was no going back and fixing this. There had been too much pain and too much loss.

"Getting my degree and coming back here gave me some satisfaction. I see Alice married her second choice."

The former cocaptain of the basketball team, Jake knew. The marriage hadn't lasted. Rumor had it that Alice had not been faithful.

"They had a daughter, too."

"I helped deliver her," she said.

He could only imagine how awkward that must have been.

"Really?"

"Don't worry, Jake, I'm doing fine. Looking out for my sisters and giving them some stability. Turns out I don't need you after all."

Was that another reason for her return? To show him that she'd succeeded despite her mother and her family—and him?

"I heard you've joined the Turquoise Guardians."

She turned back to face him. "I'll bet that sticks in your craw."

"Congratulations."

She pinned him with a hard gaze. "This isn't a game, Jake. It's my life."

"I'd like to be a part of it."

"Is this about me or about a way for you to keep Fortune?"

"Both."

She sighed. "How romantic. Funny how you only seem to notice me when there's a baby around."

"Be reasonable."

"I am reasonable. I'm trying hard not to fall in love with this baby because I know that one day soon the tribe will come and take her away from me. We aren't the parents."

"But we could be."

She blinked. "This baby has a mother."

"Who doesn't want her."

"You don't know that. There are many reasons to leave a baby with someone you trust. She might want her back."

"If I find the mother and get her to give up rights, will you consider staying with me?"

"As what, your nanny? I have a job, Jake."

"As my wife."

Her voice went cold. "Your wife. And here we are again." She gave him that long, angry stare. "When I marry, *if* I marry, it will be to a man I love and trust. I don't trust you, Jake."

His brows lifted as he noticed that she did not say she didn't love him. Could it be that Lori's feelings for him ran deeper than desire? His mouth quirked.

"Well, I'll have to work on that."

"Fortune needs a clean diaper."

How did he prove himself trustworthy? he wondered. And how did he prove that he wanted her for the woman she was?

"Why were you outside?" she asked.

Chapter Twelve

Jake stood before the Colelay's home, just a quarter mile from his own. He had explained to Lori about Ty's early-morning visit and arranged to have Wetselline watch over Lori and Fortune while he investigated what Ty's dog had discovered.

Jake mounted the steps, crossed the flaking boards of the Colelays' back porch and knocked. A moment later, Mrs. Colelay appeared behind the torn screen door. The woman's hair hung loose and greasy around her gaunt face, and her skin had a yellow cast. He knew she could not be past forty, but the lines on her face and the many missing teeth made her appear much older.

"Good morning, Mrs. Colelay. I'd like to ask you a few questions."

From inside came the cry of a baby.

"You have a baby?" he asked.

"Yeah. He's three months. Good set of lungs on him."

Jake nodded. Mrs. Colelay was not Fortune's mother. Couldn't be.

The wail went on. "Let him go a minute. See if he falls back to sleep."

The cries went on and Jake shifted, uneasy with this style of infant care. But the cries did diminish and then stop.

"He's cutting a tooth. Can't make him happy, and he slobbers like a dog smelling cooking bacon."

Jake dived right in. "I was wondering if any of your girls are here."

She squinted at him. "Why? What have they done?"

"Nothing. I wanted to ask a question about the DARE program. About graduation. Your kids have all been through the program."

She nodded, her eyes wary.

"I just want your daughters' opinions on the ceremony."

"They's all in school 'cept Zella."

"Could you remind me of their ages?" Jake asked.

Mrs. Colelay looked up and squinted, as if calculating some difficult mathematical equation.

"Let's see now. Sammy is in seventh grade. She's thirteen. The twins are fourteen—freshmen—and Zella is fifteen. Would have been a sophomore, but..." Mrs. Colelay turned her head and raised her voice. "She's done with school." Then she directed her attention to Jake. "I think it's a boy, the way she's been moping around. She don't toughen up, she'll end up like her mama."

"Could I speak to Zella?"

"I don't know. Those folks from the clinic keep

poking round and she won't see them. Actually lit out every time they come round."

"I didn't know the clinic did that." They didn't, as far as Jake knew, and that concerned him. He planned to check that with Lori.

"They said she's got something catching. So why ain't I caught it, too? She sleeps in my bed more than I do."

Jake wondered if they meant Zella had an STD.

"Who was it coming by?"

"I don't know. Different people and those gang-bangers. Minnie Cobb, for one. She says she's friends with my girl, but Zella's never been friends with that one. My gals ain't perfect, but they knows to stay away from trash." Mrs. Colelay was rubbing her upper arms as if her skin itched. "I'll see if she'll come."

Mrs. Colelay retreated into the house, leaving Jake to look through the screen. A moment later the baby started crying again.

"Hush up now," said Mrs. Colelay. Then she was hollering for her daughter.

Jake waited and Mrs. Colelay returned. "Sorry, Jake. She lit out again."

He thanked her and was headed off the porch when he caught movement. Zella appeared at the corner of the house, pausing at the assortment of dusty plastic chairs that formed a circle in the backyard.

"Hello, Zella. Thanks for seeing me."

She nodded, big dark eyes staring at him, cautious as a filly. The girl wore an oversize sweatshirt that made her legs look like two sticks by comparison. The choice of garment and the way her hand went to her middle raised his suspicions.

"Heard you've left school."

She nodded again. "Quit my job at the pharmacy, too."

"Like to tell me why?"

"They kept coming around there. They talked to the counselor, my boss. The principal kept calling me to the office. But I didn't go. I ran instead."

"Why?"

"You know Marta Garcia?"

Jake's skin began to tingle. This was the name of the second girl to go missing. He nodded.

"She told me that they were after her, too. Only, she went back to the clinic."

"Who was after her?"

"I don't know. She said someone was following her. I know she went back to the clinic and she came over to the pharmacy with a prescription. They said she was anemic because, you know, her period was so heavy. So I filled her prescription. She said it was iron pills, but it wasn't."

"What was it?" asked Jake.

"Prenatal vitamins."

Jake's skin prickled.

"I told her, and that's when she told me about the two that was following her, and then she was gone."

Jake frowned. Her mother said that Minnie Cobb had been here looking for her daughter. "Zella, is someone after you now?"

She nodded.

"Who, Zella?"

She shrugged. "I don't know them. A man and small woman."

"Have they been here recently?"

"Not anymore. They were only…"

"Only what?"

"I don't have her anymore." She looked up at him with wide, frightened eyes.

"The baby?"

"They're after her. I knew they would be. That's why I gave it to you."

"Zella, you put that newborn in my truck?"

She lowered her head and nodded.

"That little girl is your baby?"

She shook her head with vehemence and met his shocked stare.

"Did you deliver that baby?"

Another nod, jerky this time, and her shoulders began to shake.

"By yourself?"

"Yes, sir."

He still couldn't conceive how a girl with Zella's dark coloring had birthed Fortune.

"But it's not mine. I know what you have to do to have a baby and I never, ever did that with a boy."

"But that's impossible."

"It happened to Mary."

"Mary who?"

Zella pointed skyward. "Mary and Joseph."

This made no sense. But he half believed her. The

other half made him wonder if she'd snatched that baby and then panicked. Or worse, that she'd been raped. Taking her to the doctors would help determine if she had recently given birth.

"Zella, are you all right? Maybe you should come with me. Get you checked out. I could take you to the clinic."

As soon as he said *clinic*, he realized his mistake. If the tribe's health care facility was tied up in this, then he absolutely could not bring her there.

The girl backed away.

"Zella?"

She turned and ran. By the time Jake got to the corner of the property, the girl had vanished.

JAKE KNEW ZELLA could not have gone far. Behind the house was the pasture, and beyond that his home. She did not have time to cross the field, so she was close.

It took the better part of an hour to check all the places a girl as thin as Zella could hide, but he found her at last. Coaxing her out took time and patience. She made him promise not to bring her to the tribe's health clinic. Instead, he drove her to Turquoise Ridge and the series of four FEMA trailers that now comprised the tribal police headquarters. Zella sank so far down in the seat beside him as to be invisible to any passersby.

Jake met with Chief Tinnin and Detective Bear Den in the chief's trailer. Zella preceded him in and curled up in a chair, drawing her knees to her chest and pulling her sweatshirt over her legs.

"Where was she?" asked Tinnin, referring to Zella Colelay, the rail-thin, dirty female, as if the girl were a lost puppy.

"She had a sort of fort right in the bramble bushes beside her house. Blankets, chair, schoolbooks and food, of course."

Bear Den regarded the teen with hands on hips, making him look even more imposing. Zella sank farther into her seat.

Jake knew that Bear Den had been to both the school and the Colelays' residence about Zella's truancy. Bear Den had even thought she might be missing for a time, but her mother had assured him that Zella was living there, but Zella had flat-out refused to go back to school. Mrs. Colelay said Zella was too old for her to do much with.

"How'd you find her?" asked Bear Den.

"I heard her crying," said Jake.

Tinnin sat with his hands tented before him, staring across the clear surface of his battered wooden desk at Zella. "She looks like she needs a proper meal. More than one." He turned to Bear Den. "Think you could drive her over to Darabee? Maybe have your brother, Kurt, check her out without bringing her to the ER. Like to keep her reappearance quiet for now."

Jake knew that Kurt was a paramedic and worked with the air ambulance, and also volunteered at the tribe's fire department in his free time.

"Kee could do a blood test," said Jake.

Zella's knees slipped out of her sweatshirt, and she glanced at the closed door. Jake sidestepped to block any attempted escape. Zella watched him like a caged dog in an animal shelter.

Tinnin picked up the conversation. "Kee works at the tribe's clinic, son. As of right now, that makes him a suspect."

That hit Jake like a kick in the gut. He was about to protest his brother's innocence, but of course that was what anyone would do. Still, Kee was too smart to get tied up in this.

Jake thought of his brother's student loans, and fear crept into his heart.

"Kurt Bear Den is not involved," said Tinnin. "He can arrange for someone to see Zella privately. We need a blood sample from Zella, and we have one from the baby."

"The clinic has it," Bear Den reminded him.

Tinnin nodded. "Best bring the baby to Darabee, too, then."

Jake did not argue. That was the very reason he had tracked Zella. He needed answers. And he needed to know what Zella's intentions toward the baby were.

Tinnin pressed his mouth together and held Jake's gaze. "Might be safer all round to turn the baby over to Protective Services for immediate placement elsewhere."

"She was born on Turquoise Canyon land," said Jake.

Bear Den gave a nearly imperceptible nod, and Jake felt glad to have the detective's support.

"You put her under my protection," said Jake. "I'm not turning her over to you or anyone else."

"We need you back at work, Jake."

"I know that, but that baby needs me, too."

Zella watched Jake with dark, fathomless eyes. She had given Fortune to him to protect. He intended to do just that.

"Jake, you're forcing me into a bad spot."

"Aren't you investigating the disappearances of our girls? Isn't Zella a victim of a crime? Maybe they're related. Now Zella says folks from the clinic keep hounding her. And Lori has found a real connection between all the missing girls at the clinic."

"Except Weaver," said Bear Den. "She's different somehow. Seen only once at the clinic and disappeared over a month later."

Jake glanced at him but continued on. "True, but Zella received a warning from Marta Garcia that someone was after her before Marta vanished. That's why Zella hid."

Bear Den looked to Zella. "Is that true?"

Zella nodded. "A creepy couple came to the school and my house. They was looking for me."

The men regarded her.

"I think they knew I was having a baby before I did."

"How do you know that?" asked Tinnin.

"They first come after me in February," she said.

"We need to formally interview her," Jake said to Tinnin. "Get a description of the couple."

"Agreed," the chief said, then turned to Zella and asked her a question about the couple in Tonto Apache.

"I don't speak Tonto. I mean, just a little."

The three men put their heads together, speaking in low voices in Tonto.

"I'll lay odds that the creepy couple are members of the Wolf Posse. Maybe even the two who attacked the clinic," said Jake. "The gang is tied up in this, whatever it is, and this baby is the key."

"It's a big case," said Bear Den. "The kind that will help you get your gold shield."

Once, that had been Jake's goal. Now he just wanted to keep Fortune safe, and get Lori to trust him.

"I'm doing this because *I* found that baby. It's mine until someone better can convince me to let her go. That someone is not you, Bear Den, or you, Chief."

The detective's thick brows rose. Silence stretched.

"We'll bring you, Zella and the baby to the hospital in Darabee. See what they can tell us and then decide what's best," said Tinnin.

"Lori, too," said Jake.

"Fine," said Tinnin.

"And, Chief?" said Jake.

Tinnin lifted his chin and waited.

"How did it go with Kee?"

"I can't talk about that."

"Was he charged with a crime?" asked Jake.

"No."

Jake squeezed his eyes shut with relief. But then he wondered if *no* meant *no*—or just *not yet.*

Lori and the baby rode to the hospital in the back of Bear Den's SUV. The chief took point, driving Zella

Colelay. Next came Bear Den, and then Jake in the rear. If there were eyes on them, Jake didn't see them. They drove through the vacant town of Piñon Forks and then along the river to the east toward Darabee.

Kurt Bear Den met them at the entrance to Emergency, and they walked in a procession to an examination room. Detective Bear Den stationed himself in the hall outside the room. Tinnin stood watch a little farther down near the nurses' station. Jake and Lori waited in the examination room for the doctor to arrive like anxious parents.

Fortune was a good baby, but she did not like having her heel pricked and blood taken. She fussed and howled a good while, and the doctor commented on the health of her lungs.

The blood results did not take as long as Jake expected. All afternoon he'd been trying to drum up an argument convincing enough for Lori to agree to help him adopt Fortune. She had told him she needed a man she could love and trust. How did he go about earning those things? All he knew for certain was that he wanted them both—Fortune and Lori. And he didn't want Lori just because he needed a caretaker. He recognized that whatever he had with Lori, that indefinable attraction, was rare, and it was growing.

There was a knock at the door and Detective Bear Den stepped in. He said that Kurt was on his way down with the results. Detective Bear Den's brother had been the one to push the sample quickly through the in-house phlebotomy lab.

"He'll be down in a minute," said Bear Den. "You'll want to hear."

Lori gathered up the diaper bag and a small, soft blanket. "They have the results from Zella's blood test, as well?"

Bear Den nodded and said Zella had agreed to co-operate now, even seemed resigned.

"I told her that we needed her help to get her friend back. That struck a chord. She wants to help us."

"She was just afraid," said Lori, coming to Zella's defense. "Did she say who the father is?"

"Still saying she's never done that. But we know how that goes." Bear Den was used to being lied to. It came with the job. Bear Den turned to Lori. "Was Zella seen at the clinic?"

"Probably. I didn't look for her name because she wasn't one of the missing," said Lori. "But I could call Burl. He'd check for me. Then we'd know why she was seen and why they needed to follow up."

Bear Den glanced at Jake.

"Seems you were both right. The clinic is at the center of this again. We'll need to ferret out who did what."

Jake thought of Kee and issued a silent prayer that his brother had not been lured into illegality because of those massive student loans.

Lori sprang to the defense of her coworkers. "Our clinic helps our people. Keeps them from having to go over to Darabee and instead use the ER here," said Lori. "We save the tribe money and provide excellent care." She didn't sound like she was convincing even herself. She'd been the one to discover that all the missing girls had been seen at the tribe's clinic. Finally, she went silent for a moment. Then she spoke quietly, as if to herself. "I can't believe this."

"Any ideas who the couple after her were?" said Bear Den, switching subjects.

Jake nodded. "Mrs. Colelay mentioned Minnie Cobb. Said she was one of the individuals looking for Zella."

Bear Den's expression went dark. He knew Minnie and her former boyfriend, Trey Fields.

"She's seeing Earle Glass now. We'll pick them both up," said Bear Den. He shifted and his gaze went to the door, seaming anxious for the chase.

Minnie and Earl. Was this the creepy couple that Zella described? Jake had to wonder.

"And how is the Wolf Posse tied up in all this?"

He had no idea.

"Do you think I should check the records for Zella?" asked Lori.

"Too dangerous," said Jake.

"But we need that information," Bear Den spoke up.

"Either Nina or Burl could check for you," said Lori.

"Suspects," said Jake.

Detective Bear Den rested a hand over the radio clipped to his belt. "Burl was there at the shooting. So call him."

"Might still be involved," said Jake.

"He's not," said Lori.

"Call him," said the detective.

Lori lifted the phone and made the call and her request. Jake waited. Lori lifted the mouthpiece and whispered, "He's on his laptop now and checking." She lowered the phone. "Yes, I'm here."

She listened and then thanked him and disconnected.

"What did he say?" asked Bear Den.

Lori folded her arms around herself, physically shielding her body. "Zella was seen only once in January. She had a yeast infection. She did not return for her follow-up."

Bear Den did the math. "She would have been pregnant, or would that have been just before she became pregnant?"

A pall fell over the room as they each arrived at a disturbing conclusion. Lori's breath caught.

"It can't be," she whispered.

"It's possible," said Jake.

"Definitely a theory," replied Bear Den.

"By whom and for what reason?" asked Jake.

"Are you really suggesting that these girls were impregnated on our land in our clinic?" asked Lori. She did not disguise the horror in her voice.

"I'm willing to consider the possibility," said Bear Den.

"But if you're right, what would members of the Wolf Posse do with a baby?" asked Lori.

Jake made a sour face. "Sell them, maybe. There is a big market for babies."

"We can't send Zella home," said Lori. "They might still take her."

"Tinnin and I discussed that," said Bear Den. "We're taking her off the reservation."

Lori frowned. Like most of their tribe, she felt safer on tribal lands.

Bear Den continued, "I called a friend of mine for help. Gabe Cosen is chief of police up on Black Mountain. He's sending one of his guys for her. She'll be placed with a good family and be able to finish her schooling. They'll give her a new name and identity. Tell folks she's from up in Oklahoma."

Jake knew that the Apache up that way had once been on the losing side of the Apache Wars. Geronimo's band had lost to the US Army and his people, who acted as scouts. It was that decision, to fight with the United States, that gave Jake's people this land and sent Geronimo and his people to exile in Florida, and later Oklahoma.

"What about Fortune?" asked Lori. "Is Zella claiming parental rights?"

Jake held his breath.

"First of all, we don't even know if she is the girl's parent," said Bear Den. "But no, she says she just wants the baby safe and to keep it from being taken like her friend Marta Garcia,"

"She's a minor. We'll have to have her parents' permission on any release of custody," said Lori.

"If she's the mother," said Bear Den.

There was a knock on the exam door. Fortune waved her arms and gazed up at the lights on the ceiling as Bear Den verified who was at the door and emitted Chief Tinnin.

"Kurt," said the detective, moving to the door.

Lori scooped up the bassinet as Bear Den admitted Tinnin, who clicked across the crowded room followed by Kurt Bear Den, who shut the door behind him. They all gathered in a circle, their heads together over the open manila folder Kurt held.

Jake's mouth went dry as he waited. Was Zella the mother? And who was the father?

Kurt opened the folder. Jake spotted a lab-results sheet stapled to the inside.

"Got the blood results," said Kurt. "You're not going to believe this."

Chapter Thirteen

Kurt Bear Den gave the blood results to Lori as he spoke to the rest of them. She scanned the page.

"The baby's blood type is AB positive," he said.

Jake waited.

"That's a rare type. And Zella's blood type is O negative," said Kurt.

Jake glanced at Lori, who was scowling at the chart.

"That's impossible," she said.

"Why?" asked Tinnin.

Lori fielded that one. "A mother with O-negative blood cannot give birth to a child with this baby's blood type."

"The father could have AB blood," said Jake.

"Yes, but mixed with Type O, the baby might have Type A or B but not AB. Zella is not the biological mother."

"Just as she said," Tinnin murmured.

"What about the blood on Jake's truck?" asked Bear Den.

Tinnin's answer was automatic as if his mind were elsewhere. "Type O."

"Likely Zella's." Kurt glanced down at the chart. "And the blood we took from one of Jake's samples, the blood on the baby after birth, matches Zella Colelay's type. We don't do DNA tests here. You'll have to ask Jack's fiancé, Sophia Rivas, to help you with that."

Jack's woman was an FBI field agent with access to the federal government's crime labs, and it was very much looking like they were going to need them.

We are providing the FBI with samples from the scene and the infant's blood for DNA analysis. They will run it through available databases. Try for a match. I'm not hopeful. But they'll keep the information and a sample in case there is any inquiry."

Tinnin turned to Lori. "What is a possible scenario where those blood types could happen, assuming that Zella delivered this baby?"

"Well, surrogacy is the obvious explanation."

Jake felt suddenly sick. Could someone have paid Zella to be a surrogate?

"She's only fifteen," said Bear Den.

"Too young to enter into that sort of agreement," added Kurt.

"Could her mother have made this arrangement?" asked Lori.

"Maybe she didn't agree," said Tinnin, his expression troubled and his jaw working his gum with rhythmic ferocity.

"But as far as I can tell, she's only been seen at

our clinic," said Lori, and then the implications of her words struck and her mouth dropped open. Her gaze flashed to Jake. "No," she said.

Bear Den said nothing, but his expression darkened.

"I work with these people," Lori said and turned to Jake. "Your brother works there."

"Surrogacy explains the disappearances. Explains the baby and why Zella insists she's never had sex," said Bear Den. "It fits."

"You don't know that for certain," said Tinnin. "She might have been seen right here. We need more information."

"She could be lying," said Jake. "About being with a boy."

"Blood samples don't lie," said Detective Bear Den.

"We need to run the tests again," said Tinnin.

"On all blood samples," said Bear Den. "I'll call the FBI to coordinate the investigation."

"Federal involvement requires approval and an invitation from the tribal council," said Tinnin, lifting his phone from the cradle at his hip.

"What about the other girls?" asked Jake.

"We have to find them," Bear Den added.

"When did Elsie go missing?" asked Tinnin.

"November," Jake answered.

Jake counted to nine. If Elsie had been pregnant in November, she should have delivered by now—and she was still gone.

The implications settled over them all like wet, heavy snow.

Jake thought of the third missing girl, Kacey Doka. She and Colt had been serious before he enlisted. Colt had believed she'd wait, and when Jake wrote to say she'd left the reservation, Colt's letters had stopped coming. Shortly afterward, he'd been taken captive in Iraq. But now Jake thought that Kacey had not run. She'd vanished on February 22. He counted again.

If she was pregnant when she was taken then, Kacey should be ready to deliver a child. He had to tell Colt what was happening. He didn't know if it would make a difference, or get his brother to leave his self-imposed isolation, but he had to try.

Had his brother Ty known about this all along? He hoped not, but it looked like Jake needed to detain his brother for questioning. Of course, first he'd have to arrest him.

Just like he'd feared. He felt sick to his stomach.

"What's going to happen to this baby?" asked Lori.

LORI'S QUESTION HUNG in the air. What would happen to baby Fortune?

Bear Den and Tinnin exchanged looks. Kurt glanced at his brother and Jake stared at Lori.

Lori knew that under normal circumstances, the tribe would temporarily place any Apache baby with a vetted family on the rez. But this was not a normal circumstance. Someone wanted this baby badly enough to shoot at a police officer to get her. If what they said about the circumstances of Fortune's birth were true, then this baby was evidence of a crime.

They would have to interview Zella very carefully to see if she could help them determine who had done this to her. And Fortune would likely be at the center of a criminal investigation.

Lori knew all that, but she also knew that caring for Fortune was not like holding one of the dozens of babies in her care at the clinic. Fortune was much more. She'd bonded to this fair-skinned child. She was not a replacement baby. Fortune was in need of a mother, and Lori was ready to be that to her. She really didn't care what color she was. She was born here on their land. That made her their responsibility.

Lori had been trying to prove to everyone here on the rez that she could take care of herself by herself. And she owed it all to those who had pigeon-holed her, painted her with the same brush as her three older sisters and their mom. She loved her mom and her sisters, but she did not want to be like them. If not for their legacy and the girls who had been so cruel after she got pregnant, she might not have made it through her nursing program. Her fury had driven her because she would be damned if she'd fail. It just was not an option. But in her mind, she had spent too much time living in the past and too much time independently alone. Fortune kept her in the present with all the wants and needs of a newborn, and she also gave Lori connection and hope for the future.

"She'll need to be placed," said Tinnin. "You happen to know anyone who would like temporary custody of a baby?" he asked Lori.

"I would," said Jake.

All heads turned in his direction.

"I found her," he said. "She's mine."

Tinnin chewed his gum and studied his junior officer. "It don't work like that, son. Zella gave birth. She's got parental rights."

Jake pressed his lips together and faced his superior. Lori sensed a fight coming.

"Zella is the birth mother," said Tinnin.

"Surrogate," said Lori. "In Arizona that makes her the legal mother unless or until she transfers custody by adoption."

"Abandonment," added Jake. "And Bear Den said she doesn't want to keep Fortune."

"True. Zella expressed her intention to sign away her parental rights, but, as a minor, we require her mother's signature, which we don't have," said Bear Den.

"I can assign temporary custody to you both," Tinnin said.

The men looked to Lori.

Jake seemed to brace for what she might say. Her heart began banging around in her rib cage. She felt panic and something new. Was that hope? Whatever it was, it was terrifying.

"Lori?" Jake asked a question, and it contained everything in just that word. Was she with him, against him or just ready to disappear again?

She didn't want to challenge Jake for this baby,

but neither did she want to give her up. Custody with Jake raised all kinds of prickly questions that she just didn't feel ready to face. She had always been attracted to Jake. That had not changed—if anything, that attraction had grown stronger.

"Can we have a moment?" she asked.

Tinnin motioned to the hall. "Take your time. Big decision."

Lori glanced at Jake.

"I'll be right back," he said. He stepped into the hall. The men followed Jake out.

She wanted to join them but hesitated, not trusting him. What did he need to say that she could not hear? She wavered between waiting as he asked and joining them. Lori remained where she was looking down at the active little baby, wiggling and sucking on her fist, unaware of the decisions being made that would affect the rest of her life.

JAKE STOOD OUTSIDE the examination room with Tinnin, Bear Den and his brother, Kurt. Behind the closed door, Lori waited with Fortune. Jake turned to Tinnin.

"Any chance the tribe will give me full custody, if I can't convince Lori to…"

Tinnin adjusted his belt and then settled his hands on his hips. Finally, he replied with a question of his own. "What do you think?"

"I think they would prefer a couple or a woman."

"That's certain," said Kurt.

"If you want to keep that little one, you need to convince that girl to marry you," said Tinnin.

"She doesn't want me," said Jake.

"But she wants the baby," said Bear Den. His observation did not make Jake feel any better.

"You don't know that for certain," said Kurt. "She asked for a moment."

"But marriage would be better," repeated Bear Den.

"There are worse reasons to marry," said Tinnin. "Oldest reason in the world. Lots of the folks I know wouldn't have married if not for an unexpected pregnancy."

"It's a bad reason," said Jake.

"Worked out okay for me and the missus," said Tinnin, bringing all the men's attention to him. His face flushed in a rare show of being rattled. "Now, don't you go saying so or she'll chew my butt off."

No one said a word.

Tinnin cleared his throat and addressed Jake. "We'll get you set up somewhere for the night. You two mull it over and let me know tomorrow what you all decide." He turned to Bear Den. "Meantime, we need Minnie Cobb and Earle Glass in custody."

Minnie was the one who had come looking for Zella, according to Zella's mother. And Earle and Minnie were now prime suspects in the clinic shooting. Likely the "creepy couple" Zella had described.

Jake wanted more than temporary custody of Fortune. He wanted to get Lori and Fortune to safety and adopt the baby girl. Ty had told them that the

Wolf Posse was looking. That meant the officers'
homes were no longer safe. He considered going to
Ty's home, the last place anyone in the Posse would
look for them, but rejected the notion, as it could very
well get Ty killed. They were watching his mother's
home, his home and likely Lori's.

Jake raised the question with Bear Den and Tinnin.
The FBI safe house was rejected because it was off
the rez and opened up the possibility that they would
lose custody of the infant. Finally, they settled on the
best of the bad options. Tinnin would wait with the
blood evidence for the FBI while Bear Den escorted
them back to the rez.

Jake went to retrieve Lori.

"What's up?" she asked.

"Tinnin wants to give us more than a few minutes
to talk about Fortune's future placement. We have
until tomorrow. Then he'll be presenting his recom-
mendation to the tribal council." He filled her in about
the decision to involve the FBI in the investigation,
but not to use their safe house or leave the rez.

"Wise," she said.

"You want to join us?" he asked and waited while
she fell into step with him, returning to the chief and
detective.

"We need more manpower," Bear Den was saying.
"When will we have the new detective?"

"Soon, I hope. Our top candidate has accepted the
position and given two weeks' notice."

This was news to Jake. But it was easy to miss
when set against the relocation of the tribe, the ini-

tiation of the investigation with the FBI to locate the missing girls, and the usual number of domestic disputes, drunk drivers, gang violence and auto accidents.

Bear Den excused himself to retrieve his vehicle.

"We're getting a new detective?" asked Jake.

"And a new officer. Tribal council approved it," said Tinnin.

"That was fast," said Jake.

"The flood was a clincher."

"Then something good might come out of that," Lori chimed in.

"And Detective Bear Den is engaged to FBI agent Rivas," said Tinnin.

She thought of that big, intimidating man and wondered who would ever want to marry him. "Yes. I heard that. She's the FBI explosives expert Sophia Rivas. The one who set all the charges and nearly died in the blast?" asked Lori.

"That's her," Tinnin said.

"I don't really know her. She's Apache, though, isn't she?"

"Yes, she's Black Mountain Apache."

"Have they set a date?"

He shrugged a shoulder. "I doubt it. She's still recovering from injuries suffered in the blast."

Fortune squawked and Lori turned. The squawk became a cry.

She glanced at Jake. "We better go. She's hungry."

Chapter Fourteen

Thirty minutes later they arrived at the home of the brother of Officer Harold Shea. Gill worked in tribal government and was on the volunteer fire department. He had been working with their men on the move. He agreed to bunk over at his brother's if he needed a bed, but he was on hand to show them around. Though once he finished his tour of his two-bedroom home, he shoved off.

Baby Fortune had been changed and fed and now blinked at the mobile above the crib that Gill had borrowed from his mother and set up in the living room. A pink giraffe turned in a lazy circle followed by a blue lion, a mint-green elephant and a yellow zebra. They all moved to the music of a lullaby. There was also a rocking chair placed before the desk in the room that Gill used for an office. The crib and rocker looked as out of place beside the black leather sofa as a china teacup amid beer glasses.

Jake was in the kitchen cooking them up a late supper while Lori stood over the crib watching Fortune. She tried to think about how many babies she had held and fed and changed, and could not come up with a guess. There had been so many. So why did this one, looking up at the mobile with the unfocused stare of a newborn, make her heart twist? Something was happening and had been happening since she first held Fortune. Her breasts ached every time the baby nursed from her bottle. Lori had never experienced this reaction before, and there was a definite tug in her belly with the urge to hold Fortune every time she saw her.

The baby turned her head and spotted Lori, staring up at her with a look of fascination. The tug of longing grew and Lori forced herself to glance away, breaking the spell the infant cast. Lori walked to the bookshelf across the room to study the collection of objects and frowned. Gill had an odd assortment of figurines. Each showed an Indian as depicted by white culture over the years. He had a small copy of a cigar-store Indian that looked quite old and a football team mascot—a bronze chief with a full feather headdress, an exaggerated nose and a tomahawk.

Another model was of an Indian princess, her plastic breasts nearly spilling out of the painted white buckskin as she raised her arm for a perching eagle while her other hand rested on the head of the white wolf frozen in place at her side. Beside her was an Indian angel tree topper with white wings and a white-and-turquoise flowing robe that seemed a strange amalgamation of European and indigenous cultures. Her upraised hand held a dove, which was not a Native symbol of peace. Beside her was a toy from the

1950s of the TV show sidekick Tonto. This Tonto
wore his iconic headband and full plastic buckskin.

She stared down at the figure that represented all
that many whites knew of her people, the tribe name
becoming the name of a riding personal assistant for
the Lone Ranger. This toy had been on his back and
clearly was meant to sit on a horse. She knew the
horse because her older sister had once owned it. It
was a brown-and-white paint named Scout, and Lori
believed it was still in the bedroom they had shared.
She wondered if Gill would like it.

"Hmm. Hello, Kemosabi," she said to it. He continued to stare up at her with a somber, stoic expression.

She moved from the shelf and returned her gaze to
Fortune, whose eyes were closed, her features slack.
Lori flicked off the mobile and laid a mint-green blanket over Fortune's legs and belly. She had knit this
with her mother in those frightening months between
when she had told her mother that she had gotten
pregnant and the day she went to the hospital. Her
mother had been delighted, which only reinforced
Jake's belief that Lori had somehow set him up. When
had he taken the blanket?

Lori glanced down at Fortune. She was already
looking forward to when the baby woke, so she could
hold her again.

When she turned, it was to find Jake leaning
against the doorjamb between the kitchen and living
room, relaxed, arms folded, a sad smile on his full
mouth. She startled and then returned his smile, feeling a wistfulness mingle with the longing.

"Sleeping?" he said, his voice low.

She nodded and he stepped into the room, filling the space and making her heart pound. Why did her body react so to him? He was still the only one who made her brain go haywire when he got too close. It was yet another reason to keep him at arm's length. But if they were to be Fortune's parents, that would no longer be possible.

Jake stopped beside her, staring down at the little sleeping girl, and he leaned so that his shoulder touched hers as they stood side by side.

"Do you ever think about her?" he asked.

Her throat began to close. She knew exactly who he meant. Somehow she managed to reply.

"Every day."

"Me, too. She'd be almost five."

He was calculating from the time she should have been born rather than her actual birthday, three months too soon. Lori did that devil's math all the time. She'd be in preschool. She'd be attending her first powwow, her third birthday and, this year, kindergarten. The invisible ghost girl who lived with her still, growing older only in her mind and, apparently, in Jake's.

Lori leaned against Jake and he turned toward her. He gathered her up in his arms and rested his chin on the top of her head.

He rocked her gently back and forth, then he dragged in a breath and set her aside.

"Come on. I made two frozen pizzas."

She resisted grasping for his arm as he slipped away. "Sounds good."

"Plus fruit cocktail."

It was an odd addition, but Lori was past starving, and the aroma of sausage made her mouth water.

He held out his hand and she took it, allowing him to lead her to the unfamiliar dining table set for two with a candle in the middle of the table, the sort you find in grocery stores in a glass cylinder with a saint depicted on the front. A prayer candle. How appropriate.

But simply lighting a vigil candle against the darkness did not gain God's favor. At least not for her.

"I found it on the windowsill," he said, noting the direction of her attention.

She had lighted more than a few of those for their daughter.

He must have been watching her.

"I used to see your old Subaru parked at church before you left for school. I came in a few times."

She glanced up from the candle and gaped. "I didn't see you."

"I should have let you see me. We should have talked about her."

Lori's gaze slipped away as the guilt rose again. What was he doing? Was this about them, or Fortune, or the child they had buried? It was all blurring together.

"Sometimes I'd sit just two rows behind you." He went to the oven and used a dish towel to remove the pizzas, then rested them on the stove top. He brought the fruit cocktail and a plate holding baby carrot sticks and celery hunks. As he turned to head back to the kitchen, she grasped his wrist. He paused and turned to face her, standing beside her chair.

"I was hurt when you disappeared, Jake. I was grieving and I thought you were celebrating your near miss."

He shook his head. "No, I was grieving, too. I was scared, you know, worried about being able to support you both. But it wasn't until she was gone that I realized I wanted her. I wanted her..." He reached for her shoulder and then froze, fisted his hand as it dropped to his side.

"Jake?"

He shook his head, his mouth closing into a tight line.

He returned to the kitchen and carried one pizza after the other, then rested them on the pine table and handed her the pizza wheel. She stood to cut the crust into six relatively even pieces of the sausage and peppers and then turned to the cheese-and-pepperoni pizza.

Jake used the spatula to give her one of each. Lori looked down at the pizza and the strings of mozzarella that clung to the edge of the plate like a tether rope. Suddenly she did not feel very hungry.

She gave him a nudge back to the conversation. "You wanted her..."

"My dad and mom, they married early. That's why she was so dead set against it. She felt forced to marry, and her marriage was bad. But after Dad went away, I tried really hard to make her happy. You know, proud." Jake lifted his pizza slice and blew on the hot cheese before taking a bite. "Oh!" He reached for the glass of water and gulped. "Still too hot."

Lori was aware that Jake's father had been in prison and was now behind bars again for a long stretch for yet another robbery. She remembered him. He was a big man like Ty and Jake, and she knew he had hit their mother at least once. But it was never just once, she thought. She knew because Jake had told her, and he had also told her that he'd been the one to call the police on his father. But his mother had not pressed charges, and his dad was back home the next day. When he was finally locked up, it seemed the entire family breathed a sigh of relief. Unfortunately, Ty was involved in the robbery and had quickly agreed to military service to avoid joining his father in prison.

Jake had told her many things that night, bared his heart and his soul. He'd been sad and lonely, and she'd been with the boy she'd loved all her life. She would have done anything he asked, and she had. In doing so, she'd proved his mother's opinion of her was correct, having sex with her son on their first date and getting pregnant. It didn't matter that she loved him or that she'd never had sex before. What mattered was that she was just like her mother and sisters, according to Mrs. Redhorse. She could bear that, but not that Jake bought into her opinion. He'd been young. He'd been scared. But he knew how it had happened.

She tried to keep her comments positive, although

just the mention of his mother had her stomach squeezing tight.

Lori turned her attention to the meal and polished off three slices. Jake handled double that as she switched to the fruit and fresh veggies.

"I never should have listened to them, Lori. My mother, my brother Ty, my stupid friends. They were all wrong about you, about everything."

She lifted her attention from her plate and stared at him, hardly believing her ears.

"Were they?"

"Yes. You're a good woman, and you work hard. You're smart and kind and so good with Fortune."

She waited for him to tell her that he and she might have made mistakes, but their daughter was not one of them. He didn't.

"Thank you," she said and rose to clear her place and discard the paper plate and napkin.

He washed the few dishes as she put away the leftovers.

"You want to go settle in while I put these away?" he asked, motioning to the dishes. Was he avoiding talking about Fortune's future? Tinnin said they had only until tomorrow to work things out.

"Sure."

"You take Gill's bedroom. He said to tell you that he changed the sheets. I'll take the couch."

"You need blankets?"

"They're out there, I think."

She glanced toward the couch and found the pile of bedding. Then she checked on the baby, who was still sleeping, before going to Gill's room to unpack. Lori changed into her cotton nightgown and matching robe. She used the bathroom, washing up and preparing to grab a few hours' sleep before Fortune woke again.

When she emerged, she checked the baby again—finding her still fast asleep in her crib. Then she went to find Jake and confront the topic of Fortune's temporary placement. She planned to suggest that she take custody and he come around to visit Fortune when he could. After all, the tribal police department was short-staffed and the tribe needed every one of their officers. They also needed her at the clinic. But going back there now made her feel afraid. What was going on there?

She headed out to find Jake. He was in the living room. She watched him fold a sheet in two and then lay it on the long couch. He'd changed, as well. He now wore sweatpants and a muscle shirt that showed he was spending time at the police station's weight room. The sight of all that male muscle brought her to a stop.

He straightened and smiled as his gaze swept over her. "You look ready for bed."

She glanced at the open robe and the nightgown that ended at her knees. Somehow both sets of their bare feet made her feel more exposed. His were broad and brown with a dusting of hair across the tops of his toes. His sweatpants were not tight and it seemed that he wore nothing beneath them, and that information was playing havoc on her senses.

It was happening again. The internal tide was rushing, and her body made demands that she knew were foolish. Had the past few years taught her nothing?

Jake shifted from one foot to the other. "Lori, maybe it's time that we stop thinking about the past and start thinking about the future."

Chapter Fifteen

One long-ago night, when they were teens, they had taken his truck out to a quiet spot on the river and lain out on a blanket under a scattering of stars. Lori and Jake had explored each other's bodies on that moonless night. As a result, neither of them had ever seen the other one naked. She wanted that now.

She forced herself to break her gaze and the long, intimate silence by grabbing the blanket and down comforter, helping him drape the blanket over the couch on which he would sleep. She should leave now, before they touched. And they would touch. Lori was certain, because neither one of them could control themselves.

"It was nice of Gill to let us use his place." She tried to avoid the nearness of him, but her gaze slipped against her will to watch the muscles of his arm and shoulder glide and bunch as he smoothed the bedding.

A couch with clean sheets fresh and waiting.

"It was," he said. Jake set the pillow against the armrest. She laid the comforter on the bed and pictured them beneath it.

When she straightened, it was to find him staring at her with a scorching look that brought every nerve to life.

"Jake?"

"I can't stop thinking about you, Lori."

"Yes?" Somehow she'd prevented herself from telling him that she had thought of him as well, long and often.

"That night. You know? Even before that, we were friends. It made things different. I could tell you anything. I didn't have that with anyone else."

And he had told her things. All about Ty's troubles and Kee's operation and his mother and father's terrible marriage and how his father frightened him. There was no doubt in her mind that he had become a police officer to protect families from men like his father. He'd been too young to stop his dad. He hadn't left for school like Kee or joined a gang to find a new family like Ty. He'd stayed with his mother until his dad went to prison and May had a new man in her life. Now he came around to help with the things neither of them could manage. He was a good son, making everyone proud of him from the time he first stepped on the basketball court to his graduation last year from the Arizona police academy. He'd made only one misstep. With her.

"What about Alice? You never talked to her?" she asked, mentioning the girl everyone had thought he would marry.

He snorted. "Alice liked to talk about herself, mostly."

His smile held a wistfulness that made her heart

ache. Was he remembering Alice, his longtime girlfriend, and how, after he'd stumbled with Lori, the
most popular girl in high school would not even look
at him, let alone forgive him?

"Alice was never much for looking back. She was
all about the moment and the next good time."

"Do you hear from her?"

"Indirectly. Her younger brother tells me she and
her daughter live in Tucson with her new husband.
She's expecting another child."

"Imagine that."

Lori wondered if Jake was thinking that he might,
by now, be Alice's husband and a father, had Lori
and Jake not taken their intimacy to a physical place.

She flushed, recalling how neither of them had
counted on the heat they generated after just one simple kiss. Jake had not known that she had been taken
with him since grade school and over the years had
done everything she could think of to move them
from friends to something more.

She'd been so elated when he had finally broken
it off with Alice and asked her out, and so crazy in
love with Jake, that she never stopped to wonder why
he'd left his old girlfriend and chosen her until Alice
announced to her in front of half the school in the
school auditorium that it was because she wouldn't
put out and everyone knew that Lori would. Lori had
been so shocked that she didn't say anything. And the
worst part was that Lori already had "put out" and
was pregnant as a result. More terrible still, some tiny
fragile part of her brain wondered if Alice was right.

She'd felt so stupid. So little. Like she was nothing at all. She never wanted to feel like that again, and after she lost their baby, Lori swore she never would.

Jake rested his hands gently on her shoulders. The sensual brush of his index finger on her neck warmed her and sent electric charges firing down her arms and across her chest. Her breasts ached in a reaction she knew but had not felt since he last touched her.

Why did it have to be him? Why the golden boy, three-sport captain, local hero and peace officer? Why did she have to be his mistake?

He bent to kiss her forehead, his lips warm as they lingered on her. She closed her eyes and prayed for the intimacy they had shared and lost. When he drew back, she followed, looping her arms around his neck and lifting her chin, welcoming a real kiss.

"Lori?"

"Kiss me," she said. Lori was doing it again. Demanding his touch, taking all she could. Had it been all her fault?

He held back, finally nodding. "Yes."

His gaze dropped to her mouth.

Lori lifted on her toes to press her lips to his. His mouth glided over hers, stirring and rousing her, bringing her back to that place of heat and sensation.

She reached between them and tugged at the string holding his pants. They fell, and he stepped clear of them. She pulled back. He followed until she was on her back on the couch and he was looming over her. He moved lower, kissing the tops of her shoulders, and then lower still, taking his time and rousing her to a frenzy. He reached her inner thighs and she thought she might shatter. Jake Redhorse did not stop until she did just that. Sensation swirled and built inside her. She arched back and let herself go, spilling over the edge as she called his name.

He let her rest a bit as he toyed with her, his fingers grazing her stomach with feathery strokes that relaxed her at first and then aroused as her body came to life again. His kisses began once more, first at her ribs and then moving upward until he sucked at her breast as his other hand moved to tease and tug at her nipple. She was panting when his mouth finally reached hers.

"That was wonderful," she whispered. He kissed her neck as he pressed his arousal to her leg and bent her knee to increase the pressure, even as her body thrummed with the need to feel him inside her.

"Jake, now. Please."

He stilled and then reached for something. She waited as he rummaged in his discarded pants and knew what he was doing. The responsible thing.

"I'm on birth control," she said.

"No mistakes this time," he said and ripped the foil packet.

A mistake—their child. She stiffened and opened her mouth to raise an objection. To try to put into words the fury and the pain. But there was nothing, no way to explain what she felt.

"Besides, you're killing me. This will help me make this last, and that's what I want."

He fit the condom and smoothed it over the long, delicious length of him, then turned back to her.

"Lori?"

She struggled as her arousal crashed against her fury.

"What's wrong?"

"Nothing and everything," she said.

He wrapped her in his arms and held her. His scent and the contact of the warm velvet of his skin made her flesh tingle.

"It's all right," he said. "We can stop."

But she couldn't. And she knew that this one night was her chance to have Jake as the man he had become. They were no longer teens fumbling in the dark. Here was her chance to see if Jake was all she remembered, or if what they had once shared was over.

She lifted her chin and smiled.

"We never could before," she said.

They kissed deeply, his tongue gliding against hers, and she forgot all the reasons this was such a bad idea. She gave herself the gift she had longed for—the touch of a man whom she had once adored.

Lori closed her eyes to better feel him moving over her and let her legs drop open in welcome. But he called to her, made her look up into his soulful dark eyes as he glided inside, connecting them in a way that, despite all her efforts, had never really died.

She savored the velvety texture of his skin on hers and the low, throbbing want deep inside herself that he satisfied with each stroke. He gazed down at her, his eyes burning with passion as his nostrils flared. Jake was the picture of feral desire. She raked her nails down his chest. He threw his head back and dropped deeper inside her, taking them both to the brink. She arched up into the breaking wave of sensation, and he followed an instant later. They held each other through the rippling beat of release. He collapsed upon her for just a moment. She tried to wrap her arms about him, but he rolled away, one hand on himself as he made certain the protective sheath came with him.

No mistakes, she thought.

She lay on her side next to him on the wide leather couch as the cool air chilled her skin, listening to his labored breathing, and she realized that little had changed except he was more cautious now. The desire and passion were stronger than before. But Jake did not want her pregnant, and he even wanted a double layer of protection.

And she did not forgive him for thinking of their daughter as a mistake.

She threw an arm over her eyes, not wanting to look at him. The scent of their coupling now turned her stomach. What was she doing here? He would break her heart again, and she was only helping him do that.

"That was amazing," he said.

An amazingly bad choice, she thought.

"Lori?" He rolled to his side to face her. "Are you crying?"

She drew her arm away. "What are we doing?"

He shook his head, seeming confused. His brow knit. "What do you mean?"

"We're here to care for that baby and figure out what Tinnin should ask the tribal council regarding her placement, not to drop back into this again."

"This?"

"Sleeping together. This won't make us a couple or fix what is broken between us. You don't have feelings for me, Jake. If you did, you would have hung around after the funeral, tried to patch things up. But this time you should know better. I know that I sure as heck should." She pushed herself to a sitting position and snatched up her discarded nightie, then dragged it over her head.

"I have feelings for you, Lori."

She snorted. "Is that so?"

She drew her knees to her chest and pressed her hands to her forehead, tenting them over her brow, shading her eyes. It was all she could do not to rock back and forth like a weeping child. But she managed to keep from crying.

"You wouldn't see me or speak to me..." Her words were muffled and just as tangled as her thoughts.

He touched her forearm. "What, Lori?"

She dropped her hand, and he blinked at seeing her eyes gone red and the tears testing the edges of her lower lids.

"Your mother blamed me. The school blamed me. Your friends blamed me. And I sure as heck blamed myself. But I wasn't alone, Jake. You were there, too."

"I realized that, Lori."

"All these years we have never spoken about it, about her." The tears streamed down her face. "You hurt me, Jake."

"I never intended that," he said.

"I loved you. I set the moon on you. I would have done anything to make you happy. Even this," she said, motioning to the blankets tangled about them.

His eyes widened.

"I didn't trap you," she said. "You know as well as I do that you asked me out, and that night you didn't control yourself, like you told me you could."

"That's true."

"Yet when it happened and I told you, you didn't stand with me."

"I asked you to marry me."

"You did." And the entire episode made her cold inside.

"I'm sorry, Lori."

"Sorry you got me pregnant, you mean."

"No. I'm sorry I hurt you. But I would have been there for you and for our baby."

"Because it was the right thing, and Jake Redhorse always does the right thing—well, almost always."

"I told my mother that I would marry you against her wishes. What exactly didn't I do?"

"Waiting was the smart choice. You were always smart, Jake. Tactical. That way you could make sure it was yours. Was that your idea or Ty's? And did Kee suggest a paternity test or was it your mom?"

He looked away, breaking the connection of their gazes.

"She was mine, Lori. I didn't need a test."

"Waiting made all your friends think you weren't sure."

He gaped at her as if this never occurred to him.

"That's not why I waited," he said to the floor.

"No?"

"Ty told me not to marry you. So did my mother. Just provide support. Ty did suggest a paternity test. I didn't need one. I knew you, Lori. I knew it was the right thing to do."

"You always did."

"But I needed... It was an excuse. A stay of sentence."

"Sentence?" She heard the hard, dangerous edge in her voice.

"Yeah." He rubbed his neck, still not looking at her.

"Putting it off was...stupid."

"Cruel," she added. "I almost dropped out of high school. Did you know that? The girls were so horrible to me. Then we buried our daughter and you disappeared."

"I was right here." He retrieved his sweatpants and slipped them on, sitting beside her.

"You didn't want to see me."

"Lori, after the funeral, you told me to stay away from you. You said you never wanted to see me again."

She remembered screaming at him at the hospital and then at the funeral after they'd lowered the coffin into the rocky ground, the pain and rage tumbling inside her like a rock slide. She did not remember what she had said. Had she told him to leave her alone?

"I did as you asked."

"And all this time, what, you've been waiting for me?"

"Yes, in a way," he said. "I was waiting for you to move on, move forward or come back and find me again, to look at me once the way you did back then."

Now it was her turn to stare blankly at him.

"If you want me to apologize for my mother's words or the actions of the kids we went to high school with, I will. I'm sorry they were stupid and cruel and spiteful. I'm sorry I didn't stand up for you where and when you expected me to, or tell them all that I was the one who suggested we lay that blanket in the back of the truck. That I was the one who said I knew what I was doing when I didn't. And I'm sorry I hurt you."

She dropped her gaze. Her head was throbbing and her insides knotted. "It hurt that you didn't have feelings for me. I needed more than responsibility and regret."

"I would handle it differently now, Lori. We were both kids. Sixteen-year-old kids. We made some mistakes."

And there it was again.

"Do you know what it was like to be Jake Redhorse's only mistake?"

His brows descended as confusion dawned in his expression.

"No, you don't. You've never disappointed anyone," she said. "Exceeded expectations, made everyone proud. Except that one time. Proves you're human. Right? You made a mistake. Me."

"Lori, that's not how it was."

"That was exactly how it was. I never disappointed anyone. Do you know why? Because no one ever expected anything. I should thank you. You and everyone else who let me know just what they thought of me. Of us. It gave me the kick I needed to prove you all wrong."

"I'm sorry, Lori."

Her voice turned shrill. "I don't want to hear an apology. To hear how sorry you are that we got pregnant or had a child or that our baby died. I want you to acknowledge aloud that *we* were not a mistake and *she* was not a mistake."

He stared at her in shock, his mouth hanging open.

She covered her eyes with one hand and let her head drop.

Jake placed a hand on her back and rubbed. "I'm not sorry for her. Only for the pain our situation caused you. Can you forgive me?"

Could she?

"I can try." She lifted her hand just enough to see his face.

He gave her a sad, tight smile.

"I need to check on Fortune," she said.

He let her go, following only with his eyes.

They had been good friends before this all happened, starting way back in elementary school. In high school, Lori had been so smart, helping him with math, and he found himself looking forward to seeing her at school. She was the best part of his day. Then he'd finally drummed up enough courage to take her hand and he'd known right there that the connection wasn't friendship. It was too raw and visceral. He had been young, but in that moment he knew the difference between Lori and Alice. Alice was a human girl trophy, something to be won because she was the best, most popular girl in their school. Lori wasn't popular, but she was real and kind and funny and smart. And the feelings she stirred were different, deeper, real. She wasn't a prize. She made him recognize how superficial his relationship with Alice really had been and so he broke it off with her and she had not taken it well, especially not when she figured out who that other girl had been. He had let things get out of hand. He and Lori had sprung from friends to lovers too fast. Like a mudslide after the monsoons in August. Things had just broken loose and come crashing down around them in a huge, dangerous mess.

He'd let her go. But he never let her out of his sight for long. And he'd been checking on her since she came back to the rez. Driving by the clinic lot to spot her car. Noting when it was gone. Timing his visits to the diner to coincide with hers. Being disappointed when it was Nina or Burl or Verna who picked up lunch. Checking when her light went off in her bedroom window at night after he was on a call.

He'd been following her around since grade school and he'd never stopped. Jake got up and followed her down the hall.

Lori felt his presence fill up the room, but she ignored him as she clutched the crib rail and bent to look into the crib. The infant slept peacefully, her head turned to the side, her fist pressed to her cheek.

"We were almost parents once," he said from just behind her. "Now we are again."

"Temporarily," she reminded him. "Caretakers. Protectors."

He reached out and stroked Fortune's arm.

"She's not ours, Jake. We can't keep her."

"Why not? She's not a missing infant. Zella doesn't want her, her mother doesn't want her. Why can't we keep her?"

"We just can't."

"Because…?"

"Jake." Her voice held a note of cajoling and also indulgence. "She's white."

"So?"

"We don't let our children get adopted by families who aren't indigenous because we don't want them separated from their culture. Isn't this the same thing?"

He stared down at the sleeping infant. "It's not the same. She was born to a member of our tribe, for one thing. Our people used to adopt children to replace the ones that were lost. We've lost a child."

"They also took captives from neighboring tribes to replace their losses. Will you advocate that, too?"

He turned to her, looking so fierce that she stepped back.

"I'm keeping her unless our tribal court says otherwise. You can blame me for whatever you want, Lori. But I'm determined."

She blinked at him.

"We can't have our baby. But we can have this one and other ones."

"Is that why you slept with me, to convince me to help you raise this baby?"

He glared at her. "You don't get it, do you? I'm tired of tiptoeing around you, Lori, waiting for you to forgive me or notice me again. I'm tired of dating good women and finding them lacking because they are not you. But if you don't want me, I'll settle for someone who does. I'll find this girl a mother one way or another."

The anger inside her vaporized into alarm.

"You can't go out and just marry anybody," she said.

"Watch me." He stormed from the room.

She followed him as far as the hall. He turned back and met her gaze.

"All this time we could have been starting again. We could have had a child or two, a home, a life. Instead, we have regrets and grievances. I'm done with that."

He turned back around and walked away from her, switching to Tonto Apache, where his words turned to curses.

Chapter Sixteen

Lori woke for no reason she could tell and listened. The sound of a baby's early vocalizations reached her. She slipped from the bed in her nightgown and headed for Fortune's room. She had already fed her twice during the night. A glance at the clock beside the bed told her it was closer to seven o'clock in the morning than six, and the light of day was already filtering through the curtains.

She stopped over the crib to see Fortune gurgling and chirping like a baby bird.

"How's my girl?" said Lori, and then she stopped herself. This baby was not hers.

Fortune did not know this, of course, and now smiled up at Lori in a way that melted her heart. She stroked a thumb over the downy wisps of hair, admiring the shape of Fortune's head, now that her skull was recovering somewhat from the delivery. The longing and regret were powerful today. Why was she already anticipating the end of all this?

Jake wanted them to keep Fortune. Lori let herself imagine how that would look. A marriage for the sake of this child instead of the one she had borne? A partnership centered on caring for Fortune? Or possibly a second chance.

Her heart ached with yearning as she stood over the crib. Jake wanted Fortune and he wanted Lori, too. But for the baby, she reminded herself, because to think otherwise was to open herself to yet another heartbreak. A man should only be allowed to do something like that to a woman once. She'd be foolish to let him get close enough to her heart to strike another critical blow. Yet here she was, picturing the entire thing in her mind.

They'd had sex. He had apologized, and now she wondered if he had anything more to ask forgiveness for than she did. He had not said he loved her, or that he had ever loved her.

He said he had been waiting for her to forgive him, and in the next breath he'd said he wouldn't wait anymore and was moving on. Not exactly a proclamation of undying love.

She couldn't stay forever with this baby and Jake. Eventually, she'd have to go back to her life and he to his. Unless they reached an arrangement.

"Hey there." Jake's voice rumbled through her like a rising storm. She turned to see him already dressed in his uniform, his wet hair in two braids that lay on each broad shoulder. He was the picture of a man in uniform, with a clean-shaven jaw that accentuated his wide, sensual mouth. They should use him on a recruitment poster for the police force.

"Good morning," she said, offering him a smile.

Today she felt unsure around him, uncertain of how to proceed or where their relationship was heading. But she was no longer angry.

She'd carried that resentment tucked up under her heart for so long that she now felt like a hermit crab that had lost its shell. There was nothing to shield her anymore from his dark eyes or his charming smile.

He stepped up beside her at the crib and glanced at Fortune, who kicked and flailed in delight. Jake placed a broad hand around the infant's body and rubbed her belly.

"There she is," he cooed. "There's my girl."

Lori had changed her mind about Jake's convictions to adopt Fortune. She now believed that he would somehow succeed in becoming the baby's father. There was still some question on whether she would be included in his newly forming family. She swallowed as she recognized the startling emotion rising up inside her, fragile as a soap bubble. Was that hope?

Jake turned his attention to her. "How are you?"

She nodded, not trusting her voice. Lori cleared her throat. "I'm, you know, adjusting."

He made a sound in his throat. "Yeah. It's a lot."

"Yeah."

"But good, too. You know, I was ready to be a father five years ago."

"I know."

"Will you help me keep her, Lori?"

She wanted him to tell her he loved her and that he wanted to try again. Helping him could run the gamut between changing a diaper to speaking on his behalf before the tribal council.

And she realized then that she would do whatever he needed to help him keep this baby because it was right. He was meant to be Fortune's dad. "I'll help you, Jake."

He leaned in and kissed her on the cheek. He smelled like shaving cream and mint toothpaste. Lori inhaled deeply. Jake stepped away and headed for the door. "I've got to get my other bag from my unit. Then I'll make us pancakes."

Jake whistled down the hallway. She heard the front door click open and closed. Lori turned to Fortune, who was doing a nice job kicking the air.

"Come on, my girl. Let's get you cleaned up."

She got the baby changed and dressed. Thanks to Carol Dorset, the tribe's dispatcher, she had plenty of baby things. Carol was a grandmother many times over and had easily assembled the necessary items.

"You hungry?" Lori asked Fortune as they headed down the hall and into the kitchen.

Lori reached the kitchen and stood at the sink, glancing out at the backyard when she heard a male voice shouting from outside of the house. She moved through the kitchen toward the front door, thinking Jake had called her name, an instant before the back door burst open. Lori's gaze fell on a petite woman dressed in a yellow satin sports jacket, tight black jeans and sneakers with the laces tucked but not tied. On her head sat a black satin ball cap turned sideways. Above the brim was a glittering gold display of a royal flush. Her eyes were covered with wide, dark sunglasses, and the lower half of her face was draped in a black bandanna. Lori recognized the colors of the tribe's only gang—the Wolf Posse.

Was this the same woman from the hospital?

She had a similar slight build. Lori's heartbeat tripled as she faced the woman. She thought she could take her, but not with Fortune in her arms. Lori backed into the living room as a man stepped in behind the woman. He, too, was dressed all in black and wore sunglasses and a hat tugged low over his forehead, a bandanna covering the bottom half of his face. His dark hair hung loose past his shoulders. In the opening of his coat, she glimpsed a breastplate, reminiscent of the ones worn by the warriors of the Great Plains, but instead of horizontal rows of finger beads, this regalia had been constructed of what looked like copper tubing, joined with metal beads and embellished with yellow cording.

Lori backed toward the front door.

"Hand her over," the man said to Lori.

Lori continued her retreat.

"Where's the cop?" asked the woman.

"Grab the kid," he said to his partner.

Lori did not take time to think. She screamed. Then she turned and ran, heading toward the front door. Lori prayed the door would not be locked. Her hand was on the knob.

"Get her!" shouted the woman.

The footsteps pounded across the room as she wrestled with the knob. Jake's face filled the small window in the door. Something crashed behind her. Lori stepped back as the front door swung open. Jake stood on the concrete step, his service pistol out and aimed down. He reached forward and dragged Lori, still clutching the baby, through the door, then stepped before her, shielding her with his body.

The concrete was freezing against her bare feet. The morning breeze fluttered her nightie about her naked legs. She huddled around Fortune, shielding the baby from the wind. Above her, Jake now filled the open doorway.

"Police!" he yelled in a voice she had never heard before. It rang with authority and scared her almost as much as the intruders had.

She could not see the couple in the house as she instinctively moved away from Jake and crouched beside the foundation, curling herself around the newborn. Her shoulder hit the concrete block wall, abrading her bare shoulder and jarring her teeth. She glanced up as Jake lifted his pistol.

"Gun!" he shouted and fired.

His gunshot reverberated through her chest and made her ears ring. A spent cartridge pinged on the concrete walkway beside her and bounced away. An instant later, she heard a second shot.

Fortune wiggled and wailed in a tiny, fragile cry. Lori cradled her fuzzy blond head and pressed her lips to her forehead, making a shushing sound that she could not hear past the ringing in her ears and the slamming of doors. She caught the odor of gunpowder as Jake fell backward to his seat on the front walk.

The woman shouted. Something crashed.

Jake lifted a hand to his chest. He'd been shot. Oh, God, he'd been shot.

"Jake!" she cried.

He did not look at her but tried and failed to draw a breath. His face was scarlet. His eyes bulged. She crawled the distance that separated them and grasped at him with her free hand.

"Oh, no. Jake! Please, no."

Where are they?

She glanced to the open door and saw the empty living room and the kitchen beyond. The dinette lay on its side, as if it had been used as a barricade. One of the chairs had been upturned and tossed against the wall.

Her gaze swept along the side of the house in one direction and then the other, scanning for movement.

Her heart beat in her throat. There was no car or truck in sight on the long hill sloping down to the road. The trees now loomed ominously beyond the driveway. Were they there right now, aiming the pistol at them?

Jake's face turned toward purple, the bluish tinge taking hold of his lips.

Lori reached to the radio on Jake's utility belt and tugged it from its plastic cradle.

She depressed the button. "Officer down! Jake Redhorse. He's shot. I think he's shot. Send help. He's at Gill's house..." She was babbling, hearing the panic in her voice.

His eyes pinched closed. She had to do something.

She was a nurse. But oh, sweet heaven, she'd never had to treat someone so close to her. Where was the blood?

Lori caught movement and saw something darting between the tree trunks, racing fast and low to the ground. From the road came the sound of tires spinning on gravel. The yellow truck flashed from the tree line, past the house, continuing on toward the main road.

Jake's breath came in a shuttering, hard-won battle. The second breath was better. His face went from blue to unnaturally gray in three breaths.

"Jake?"

"Le-go the button," he whispered.

"What?"

"Radio...button." His gaze flicked from hers to the black radio she clutched.

She glanced down and released the button she was pressing so hard that her thumbnail had gone white.

An instant later she heard the voice of the dispatcher, Carol Dorset, asking for her to identify herself.

"Lori Mott. It's Lori. They shot him." She let go of the button this time.

"Sending EMS and all available units. What is the condition of Officer Redhorse? Over."

"He's breathing now. Conscious." Lori held the radio in one hand and clung to Fortune with her opposite one.

"Bleeding? Over."

"I'm not sure yet. I..." She dropped the radio to tug at the buttons of his shirt with one hand.

He lifted the radio.

"Carol, two suspects. Native American. One male, six feet, long hair, black clothing and..." He winced and dragged in a breath. Sweat beaded his forehead, but he continued speaking. "Copper breastplate. Second...female, four feet ten, dressed in black. Yellow jacket. Possibly Minnie Cobb." He released the button.

There was a pause and then Carol's voice emanated from the radio. "Vehicle? Over."

Jake looked to her. She took up the radio and described the truck.

"Got it," said Carol. "Hang on, Jake. Help's coming."

Jake sagged backward. "Lori?"

She leaned over him, cradling Fortune in the crook of her arm as she fumbled with his shirt buttons with her free hand.

"Yes?"

"I think I'm going to pass out." His eyes fluttered, and he made good on his prediction.

"No! No. Jake, don't." But his eyes rolled white and his features went slack.

He was going to die right here in front of her.

Chapter Seventeen

Lori saw the hole in the center of the left pocket of his gray police uniform shirt. The fear rose higher in her throat as she set down the baby to see to Jake. She tore the shirt open, sending buttons flying. Beneath the shirt was the nylon sheath that covered his Kevlar vest.

She gasped in surprise and relief. How had she forgotten that he always wore this? Had it stopped the shot, or was this one of those hollow-tipped bullets, the ones they called "cop killers."

She tugged at the Velcro straps at his side and lifted the warm, heavy front panel. Then she groped beneath with one hand, checking the place that matched the hole in the front of his vest. No blood. She sank back on her heels and closely examined the vest, finding the tiny hole and the hard, flattened metal that could so easily have taken him from her forever.

In that moment, she realized that she was not over Jake Redhorse. The thought of losing him to a bullet crystallized everything. She had fought to prove herself and to prevent herself from again experiencing the pain only he could cause her. But insulating from future hurt was no protection at all. That little flattened bit of lead had proved that to her.

It would be hard to trust him and to earn his trust. But that was the only course for her now.

Her hands were under the vest again, checking, probing for some injury. But she was breathing again, the tears no longer choking her. She pressed on the thick muscle of his chest and he groaned. His dark eyelashes lifted, and he stared straight up at the blue sky. Then his gaze shifted to her.

"Where's Fortune?" he asked.

Lori retrieved her, holding her so he could see Fortune. "She's fine."

He closed his eyes and drew a deep breath, his nostrils flaring. "That's good." He shifted and groaned, then pushed up on an elbow. "They gone?"

"Yes."

From somewhere far away, she heard the sound of a siren.

"Okay, then," he said. After a moment, he asked her to help him sit up.

She tugged and he pulled, and they got him to a sitting position. Now he'd gone greenish around the face.

"Maybe you should lie down again."

"Give me a minute." He pressed his lips together, his breathing shallow. His color did return, but it took more than a minute.

"Take the baby inside. It's too cold out here for her," he said.

Lori did as he said and then came back for him.

"I didn't hear them pull up," she said. "If you didn't call me, I might not have gotten her out."

He blinked at her in confusion. "I didn't call."

Their gazes both turned to the forest abutting the property. Who had warned her?

THEY BROUGHT JAKE by ambulance to the temporary trailers that now comprised the tribe's health clinic, where they were met by Kee. When the ambulance took over, Lori had run into the house to grab the diaper bag and thrown on the closest thing, which was her nurses' scrubs and clogs. Fortune had begun crying en route.

Betty Mills met them outside the trailers and offered to take the newborn, but Lori declined. Betty pushed her owlish glasses back on her narrow nose as Lori held the wailing child.

"Please get me a bottle of formula," said Lori.

Betty stiffened but did not move. No one but the head physician, Hector Hauser, gave Betty orders, and judging from her thunderous expression, Betty was not having it. Finally, her supervisor turned. Her staccato steps rang on the metal stairs of the trailer as she headed away.

Lori could deal with ruffled feathers later.

She glanced around the trailer's interior. She'd never been inside the portable medical facilities and was surprised to see it looked very much like the inner part of their urgent-care center, with three curtained examining rooms, one bathroom and a portable ultrasound and X-ray machine. She assumed the locked cabinets beside the small stainless-steel sink held drugs and other medical supplies. There was even a large refrigerator and a water dispenser set beside a small desk with a computer along the opposite wall.

She turned back to find Jake gripping Dr. Redhorse's wrist, which held a pair of open medical scissors as his brother tried to cut off Jake's vest.

"I have to buy the uniform and vest," Jake said. Kee gave up and Jake let him go. Kee helped him sit up, and then he assisted him in removing his shirt before releasing the Velcro straps of his body armor.

Lori scanned his upper body for injuries. She noticed the well-defined muscles that armored his chest, protecting him, she hoped, from serious harm. Her skin tingled at seeing Jake shirtless, until she saw the bruises, and then her skin went cold. Here was the visible reminder of how close Jake had come to leaving this earth. Seeing him alive and well made her fear of facing the possibility of another rejection seem a frail and feeble reason to keep from trying again with Jake.

Lori's gaze shifted to Dr. Redhorse as he examined Jake.

Kee more resembled his mother, sharing her cleft chin and dimples. He was the only Redhorse boy to have cut his hair short. He had a penetrating stare and an intelligent glint in his eyes. He stood several inches shorter than Jake because of the corrective surgery.

Betty returned, holding a small bottle. "I have three of my own, Lori. I think I could feed her."

Lori did not disagree but took the formula and offered Betty sincere thanks. Betty watched her shift the infant to the crook of her arm and expertly offer the bottle.

"We have a women's health trailer, including a delivery room and nursery. I can take the little one over there. Nina is working. She'll take care of her."

Lori felt the weariness settle in her shoulders and lower back. But she was not leaving Jake or this baby.

Betty held out her hands. "Come on. Pass her over."

She was saved from a reply by the appearance of Detective Bear Den.

"Jake?" he said. "That truck. Did it have black pinstriping?"

"Didn't see it." Jake now lay on his back on the examining room table. "Lori did."

The detective swung his attention to her. She took a reflexive step back and shook her head.

"I only saw it for a second and through the trees."

"Any pinstriping?" Bear Den asked again.

Lori shook her head. "I don't know."

"What kind of yellow? Mustard?"

"No. Bright yellow, like daffodil or lemon."

Bear Den's gaze shifted to Betty Mills, whose ears had perked up.

"We'll call you if we need anything," he said, dismissing her.

She snorted. "I'll remind you that I run this clinic."

Bear Den's brow lowered, and his features turned fierce. It was obvious that the detective did not respond well to being bossed.

"And I run this investigation," he said to her. "Now get out, or I will put you out."

Betty's jaw dropped and she glared at him. Then she whirled and stormed away, her heels banging on the trailer floor.

Bear Den watched until Betty had vanished through the trailer's outer door and then swung his attention back to Lori.

"Tell me what you saw, from the beginning."

She did, relating everything she remembered in a string of babble. She had not even realized she had switched to Tonto Apache until Bear Den placed a hand on her shoulder and she remembered to breathe.

"Slow down, Lori."

She looked up at him as the fear began to gel into anger.

"Are you going to catch these two?" she asked him.

"Someone shot one of our own. You better believe this is a top priority with the force."

JAKE RARELY SAW his brother Kee ruffled, but this was the exception. Perhaps seeing his kid brother shot in the chest would do that to a person.

He seemed relieved when his longtime mentor, Dr. Hector Hauser, arrived to take over. Kee actually had to sit down beside the examining table, and for a moment there, Jake thought he'd have to give up his place.

It was Hauser who had first noticed Kee's leg-length discrepancy when his eldest brother was a boy, discovering the reason for Kee's awkward gait and inability to keep up with his younger brothers. He'd also been the one to arrange for the surgeries that evened his brother's legs. Jake thought Kee's decision to become a physician had much to do with Hauser's influence.

Lori and Detective Bear Den were speaking just beyond the open ring of curtains that encircled this exam area. He could make out only Detective Bear Den's questions and not Lori's murmured replies.

Hauser examined Jake's bare chest, noting the bruise on his skin that was ripening to the color of plums.

"Seems to be just soft tissue damage. Did they fish the lead out of your vest?"

Kee rose to do that and used forceps to retrieve the business end of the bullet from his vest. The projectile was now spread to a very flat lump of lead.

Bear Den returned. "Don't touch that," he instructed Hauser.

Hauser nodded and held the bullet out for Bear Den to collect in an evidence bag.

"Did it penetrate the other side of the vest?" Hauser asked Kee, who was up and on his feet again.

"No. It didn't." Kee's shoulders rose and fell as he blew away a long breath of relief. "Never touched him."

Detective Bear Den stepped aside as Hauser wheeled over the X-ray machine. Lead vests were placed and everyone but Jake shepherded out during the X-ray.

Then Bear Den got Jake's statement as Kee, Lori and Dr. Hauser examined the digital display.

"No fractures in evidence," Hauser said. He excused himself to see about an incoming patient.

Kee offered cold compresses for the bruising and some painkillers. He asked Lori if she wanted him to bring the baby to the nursery in the women's care trailer, and she declined again.

Kee said he'd check back and left them.

"Don't tell Ma," Jake called after him.

Kee lifted a hand, signaling that he had heard, and disappeared out the trailer door.

Lori turned to Bear Den. Some of the color had returned to her cheeks, and some of the starch to her spine.

"Why does everyone want this baby?" Lori asked the detective.

"You mean Mills and Dr. Redhorse," Bear Den said.

"No, not them." She puffed up her cheeks and blew out her frustrations. "I just mean, everyone wants her. The two who tried to snatch her from the nursery, and then the two today at the house."

"Same two, I think," said Bear Den. "Their timing was bad at the clinic. Only Burl Tsosie was supposed to be there."

They would have taken Fortune easily, Jake realized. Now it wasn't his ribs that ached, it was his heart.

"How'd those two know about Fortune so fast?" asked Lori.

Before Bear Den could address that one, she hit him with another.

"And what about the Protective Services thing? I'm certain Betty told me that she would call." Lori rubbed her chin with her thumb thoughtfully. "I'm sure."

"You think she's involved in this?"

"I didn't say that," Lori hedged.

"So then the question becomes, why did she lie?" asked Jake.

"To cover her butt, maybe," said Lori. "She's not above throwing someone under the bus when a mistake is made. I've seen that firsthand."

"What do you mean?" asked Jake.

"Nina Kenton has worked in our clinic since we opened. But when she asked Betty about a girl who was not on the appointments for Hector, Betty reprimanded her, just because she asked a question. Even put it in Nina's personnel report. I can't remember what it said, but it was a professional way of saying 'You do your job and I'll do mine.'"

"What job?" asked Bear Den.

"Scheduling. Patients and the staff. That's all Betty's job, along with medical records, billing and payroll. She is very good at what she does. Makes very few errors. But when she does make one, she rarely gets the blame."

"You don't like her," said Bear Den.

"I'm afraid of her. And she's my supervisor. Am I supposed to like her?"

Jake was lucky. He had nothing but respect for Wallace Tinnin. The man had come to his home more than once during Jake's childhood over domestic disputes, and Jake had always wished that Tinnin had been his father instead of the unpredictable, volatile man who sired him.

As if summoned by Jake's thoughts, Tinnin appeared in the trailer door and clunked down the hall on his metal crutches, drawing up at the cubicle where they gathered.

Chief Tinnin's gaze swept the curtained interior, pausing on Detective Bear Den before stopping on Jake.

"How you doing, son?" he asked Jake.

"I'm fine, sir," he replied.

A smile lifted one side of Tinnin's sagging features.

"Guess what just pulled into the parking lot?"

"Yellow truck, with black pinstriping?" asked Bear Den.

"Right in one," said Tinnin.

Lori moved to stand beside Jake.

"Any guesses as to who pulled in with a bullet wound in his stomach?"

"Faras Pike." Bear Den named the head of the Wolf Posse.

"I wish. It's Earle Glass. Hauser is outside checking him now."

Jake chuckled. The pain made him clutch his chest and reconsider. "Almost worth getting shot."

"They bringing him in here?" asked Bear Den.

"Transport to Darabee for surgery. EMTs are en route."

"What about Minnie Cobb?" asked Lori.

Tinnin's smile vanished. "Still looking."

Bear Den directed his comments to the chief. "Glass didn't act on his own, which means the gang is involved and that infant is still in danger."

"We might need to have a talk with Mr. Pike," said Tinnin.

Jake grimaced and wheezed as he slid from the table. "Where's my shirt?"

Bear Den was already heading for the door, and Jake tried to follow. Tinnin stopped him with a hand, and far too easily. Jake sagged and then groaned. He shifted, trying to find a more comfortable position but failed.

"We got the truck and Earle," said Tinnin, resuming his grip on his crutches.

"That truck belonged to Trey Fields," said Jake. "Glass say why he's driving it?"

"Says Trey told him to look after it," said the chief.

"Hmm. My understanding was that Minnie Cobb drove that truck," said Jake. "Whereabouts today?"

"Won't say," said Tinnin. "He's seventeen, so he's still a minor. I'll lay down good money that his story about accidentally shooting himself is bull, and that the bullet in his belly is a match for Redhorse's pistol. Bullet's still in there, so that's a bit of luck." Tinnin turned to Jake. "I'll need that gun, son."

Jake removed it from his holster, released the clip

and checked the chamber. Then he passed the weapon to his superior.

"All this happened while I was lying here?" asked Jake.

"Well, your bullet made it a lot easier to find Earle."

"Who is Earle Glass?" asked Lori.

"Wolf Posse member," said Tinnin. "He's been looking after Trey Fields's girl while he's away."

Jake knew that Fields had been the one who almost got FBI field agent Sophia Rivas killed by revealing her location to the Flagstaff gang, who had ordered a hit.

"Isn't he in jail?" asked Lori.

"Prison," Tinnin corrected. Most folks didn't know the difference. "Weapons charge. But he didn't buy that truck. Minnie Cobb did."

Jake knew that. He even knew the truck, but he hadn't seen it. Lori had.

"She used her Big Money," said Jake. Minnie had wasted her share of tribal revenue carefully tended for the first eighteen years of her life on her older boyfriend, Trey Fields. It was a problem among them, young girls targeted and flattered and cajoled into spending their fortune on the men who used them and then moved on to new targets. Had Minnie reclaimed her truck, or had she chosen a different companion?

"Where do you want me?" asked Jake.

"In bed. You looked like hell before you got shot, and catching lead hasn't improved your appearance."

Bear Den reappeared and approached Lori, targeting her like a heat-seeking missile. He glanced at his notes.

"Did you say you saw something moving in the woods?"

"Yes."

"Human or animal?"

"Animal, I think. It was so fast."

"Black?"

"I don't know."

Jake's stomach tightened as he put the pieces together just a little too late. The shout of warning and the moving shadow. He pinched his eyes closed but said nothing.

Bear Den continued. "A dog, maybe?"

"Could be."

"And you say someone shouted just before the pair broke in through the kitchen door?"

"Yes," said Lori. "It gave me time to escape."

Bear Den turned to Jake. "Did that warning come from you?"

Jake met the serious stare and thought for just one moment of lying to protect his brother Ty, who had a black dog and sounded very much like him.

"No," said Jake."

Bear Den nodded and then spun, heading again for the exit.

"Where's he going?" asked Lori.

Jake stared after Bear Den. "To arrest my brother Ty."

Chapter Eighteen

Kee returned to the exam area where Jake rested to report that the FBI emergency protection detail was on their way. Jake was weighing his limited options. He knew Bear Den was going to bring Ty in for questioning. He needed to be there for his brother and also be here to protect Lori and Fortune. He felt as if someone had hit him in the chest with a sledgehammer.

His radio had allowed him to follow the arrest of Minnie. She was en route to the jail in Darabee, where the new chief there had offered their facilities. The FBI were going to escort Jake and Lori to Darabee, where they would attempt to make a positive ID of Minnie. Earle had been transported to the Darabee hospital for surgery, and they would see him later today.

Kee's phone rang, and he pulled it from the cradle at his belt. His eyes widened and he met Jake's stare.

"It's Ty," he said. Kee stuck a finger in one ear and pressed his phone to the other. Jake listened, wishing Kee had put the call on speaker. Kee described Jake's injuries—bruises, soft tissue and so forth.

"He's resting," said Kee, stonewalling Ty.

Jake motioned for the phone.

Kee shook his head, his frown deepening. Was Kee protecting him from Ty, or Ty from him?

"Would you like to speak to Detective Bear Den? He's here at the clinic, and the FBI is en route."

That was a warning, Jake knew.

"Fine," said Kee, and he extended the phone. "He wants to speak to you."

Jake took the phone. "Ty?"

"Jake?"

Kee muttered something and folded his arms.

"How you doing?" asked Ty.

"I'm fine. How'd you hear so fast?"

Ty did not answer the question but instead asked one of his own. "The baby all right?"

"She's fine. Ty, Bear Den was asking me about you. Lori saw a dog."

Ty swore. "You should turn that baby over to the feds," he said.

"I'm not turning her over to anyone. I'm applying for custody with the tribe."

There was a long pause. Jake stared at Kee, who seemed to be holding his breath.

"Temporary custody?" Ty asked, his tone cautious.

"What's this about, Ty?"

"I need to know if you plan on keeping her."

The answer was an immediate yes, followed by another pause and the sound of a long intake of breath.

"All right. I'll see you soon."

"Ty? You should come in."

"Soon."

"Ty? Stay away from Pike. This is my fight."

"Jakey, you've always been able to take care of yourself. But today someone tried to put a bullet in my little brother's chest. I'm involved. Like it or not."

Jake was sure whatever Ty was planning was either illegal or dangerous or both. And he was very much afraid it involved the Wolf Posse.

"Ty, don't."

"You want that baby?"

Jake could not answer. He wanted her. But he did not want to say anything that would endanger his brother's life or force him back to the Wolf Posse. He knew how hard Ty had worked to distance himself from the gang. And he knew Faras Pike, the head of the Wolf Posse. Faras did not do favors for old friends. If Ty cut a deal over Fortune, it would cost him.

"Glad you're all right, brother."

"Ty, are you listening? Don't—"

Ty disconnected.

"What's he going to do?" asked Lori.

"I don't know." And he might never know, Jake realized.

Bear Den returned with two white males dressed in suits and sporting matching short, military-style haircuts.

The FBI had arrived.

DETECTIVE BEAR DEN waited in the Darabee police station with Lori while Jake left with Tinnin for the lineup that would include Minnie Cobb. They had arrived with the two FBI agents, who waited for them to finish. Arrangements for their housing were still ongoing.

Detective Bear Den left her with Carol Dorset, the tribe's longtime dispatcher. Someone would need to be with the baby while Lori looked at the suspects.

Lori knew and trusted Carol Dorset. The woman's somber expression transformed completely as she fussed and cooed over Fortune. Carol dyed her hair, which was still the same black as she'd been born with, but now her hair was thin, and Lori could see her scalp and the rings of flesh that hung on her thin neck like a turkey's. Carol stroked Fortune's perfect pink cheek with a swollen arthritic finger, her terracotta skin a sharp contrast to the pale pink of Fortune's tiny face.

"She's a pretty baby. Look at that hair. It has some red in it, I think."

Lori looked more closely. It seemed blond to her. "Really?"

"I think so. And she has a curl already." Carol fussed and created a curl of the wispy fluff on the newborn's forehead. "Oh, I remember when mine were this age." There was a definite ache of longing in her voice. This was followed by irritation. "I wish my son and his wife would get busy and give me another grandbaby."

The chief called for them to come in, and Detective Bear Den returned for her, filling the now-open door. The detective didn't say a word, but his expression was grim. Jake, Lori surmised, had not made a positive ID. Bear Den stepped aside and motioned to Lori. She glanced back at Fortune in her bassinet.

Bear Den motioned to the door. "Ready?"

FARAS PIKE STOOD before the big boss. He'd been thoroughly searched prior to being allowed in, including an electronic sweep by something he assumed would check for bugging devices.

"Update?" said Vitoli Volkov, his accent heavy.

Faras started to sweat. If Volkov discovered he was lied to, Faras knew he'd be killed. But he just wasn't ready to murder a newborn, and keeping his word to Ty Redhorse made this a win-win. If it didn't get him killed.

"The baby died, and the mother is still on tribal lands."

"Hmm. Disappointing. We'll report a miscarriage to the buyers. Tell them it was…damaged."

Faras wondered if he meant handicapped. Would they kill a baby who was less than perfect as some kind of hideous quality control? He didn't want to think about that.

"You have a replacement in mind?"

Faras nodded. It was simple to choose a girl who would not be missed. There were so many. Kids whose families were shit. Easy to lure. Easy to enlist. He just handpicked the girls he would have recruited for the gang and gave the Russians the ones he didn't want.

Volkov's bloodless lips twitched. "The doctor has this name?"

"The doc's already seen her. The girl's pregnant with the same donors as Zella Colelay."

"When will you bring her?" asked Volkov.

"A few weeks. Wait for this mess to die down."

"If the feds stay to snoop around that clinic, I want to know."

Faras had not mentioned the FBI to Vitoli. But he knew. That made Faras very concerned. He glanced toward the door, wishing he were gone.

"I can do that."

"I may have to move operations."

That would mean a loss of income for Faras. But it would also mean he would only answer to the dealers who supplied them with product.

"I'll wait to hear about delivery of the new girl. Don't wait so long that she tells someone she's pregnant."

"She doesn't know yet."

"Good." Volkov's gaze flashed to his man at the door, and he gave a slight nod. Faras drew a breath and held it as he waited to see if the man would reach for the door or his weapon.

Volkov's man opened the door.

The meeting was over, but Faras did not breathe easy again until he was back in his own car and heading up the mountain road toward the rez.

Chapter Nineteen

They were moved again.

Neither Lori nor Jake had made a positive ID on Minnie Cobb, and she was released from custody. Jake and Lori were then transported by the FBI to the Darabee hospital, where Lori made a positive ID on Earle Glass.

Jake and Lori were then transported to an FBI safe house, thanks to the help of Agent Luke Forrest.

He'd driven to the hospital and assigned two members of his team to escort Jake, Lori and Fortune to the ranch-style home tucked in an upscale suburb of Darabee.

The men let them into the house and set up protection. One man remained in the main living area, and the second was posted outside in the driveway in the sedan.

Food was ordered as Lori and Jake got settled and fed Fortune. Fed, changed and tucked into her bassinet, Fortune sucked on a pacifier. As her eyelids closed, the sucking became less frequent until she slept. Jake hadn't realized just how exhausted Lori was until she dozed off sitting at the table after eating her meal from a foam container. He nudged her awake.

"Let's get you to bed," said Jake.

At the mention of bed, her eyes opened wide and she bit her lower lip. A rush of heat blasted through him. Lori glanced to the agent, who was reading the paper.

"Uh, sure. All right." She lifted Fortune from her bassinet.

They left the agent on duty and headed toward the bedrooms in the back of the house.

"We each have a room," Jake said.

"I'd rather stay in the same one with you," she said.

"I'd like that, too."

His room already held his duffel bags. He left her only to retrieve her things and place them with his own. Lori had transferred Fortune to the crib provided by the bureau. He checked on her, watching her breathing as she slept on her back. The green blanket stretched across her stomach and legs and was then tucked under the crib mattress.

"The bathroom is fully stocked. You don't need a thing," she said. She motioned, showing him a large bathroom with white subway tile and an enclosed shower behind a glass door and partition. The clean, inviting bathroom made him realize how long it had been since he'd had a chance to bathe.

"That looks wonderful," he said, a note of longing evident in his voice.

"I could use a shower," she said.

"Care to join me?"

Lori's brow quirked, and she gave him a look of speculation. The heat in her gaze was unmistakable.

"Maybe I will," she said.

The quiet calm he'd felt over supper had morphed into a charged energy that buzzed between them like a field of honeybees.

"Are you tired?" she asked.

He gave a slow shake of his head.

"Not tired." She stepped forward.

His breath caught, and he began praying that he was reading this right. She stopped before him and grabbed his shirtfront, then tugged. He let her pull him against her because this was exactly where he wanted to be.

She kissed him hard on the mouth, but she didn't pull back. Instead, she tugged harder, pressing herself to him and angling her head to deepen the kiss.

Jake let it all happen, the rush of anticipation, the heat of her small, firm body rubbing up against his. When her hips made deliberate contact, he wrapped his arms around her and started backing them up. He didn't know if he could make it to the big bed down the hall, but after they showered, he was going to make love to Lori if she'd let him.

Her fingers were splayed over his chest now as they danced backward across the tile floor. She wrestled with his utility belt, which held a loaner weapon supplied by his department. She had his shirt out of his trousers now and her hand raked up his back. Her nails scored the skin across his shoulders.

He broke away from the kisses, and she redirected her sweet lips to the bare skin above the scoop of his undershirt. His head dropped back, and he closed his eyes in ecstasy and gratitude. Lori was finally in his arms again.

She stopped and her arms crossed as she clutched the hem of her blouse. A quick tug and she had it over her head, releasing the garment to let it fall behind her. In that same moment, he stripped out of his uniform shirt and the protective vest and dropped them to the floor. Only his white undershirt covered his torso.

He dragged her close. Her body molded to his, soft and warm. Her stomach was taut, with nothing to indicate she had once carried his child. He wanted another one, but only if and when she did. He wanted to talk to her and kiss her and tell her everything that was in his heart. But there would be time for that later. Wouldn't there?

She wore the sort of bra that a woman wears when she hopes something will happen, all lace and lift. He ran a finger down the hollow between her breasts, where the soft flesh crowded in together.

Lori stepped out of her clogs, and then everything else except the matching scrap of white lace that skirted across her backside and down into the cleft between her round cheeks. Jake forgot how to breathe as his body jerked and twitched as if she'd run an electrical current through him.

She turned and he stared, his gaze dipping from the high lift of that sharp chin all the way down to her small feet. Her tawny brown skin glowed with healthy pink undertones and the blush of youth. She reached behind her head and freed the tie that held her hair in a practical ponytail at the base of her slim neck. Then she shook out her hair, letting it fall around her shoulders.

Her breathing was labored and the areolae of her breasts had tightened to press against the lace.

"Your turn."

"My underwear isn't as fancy," he said.

She smiled. He felt his body pulsing, and his skin was ridiculously sensitive. He stepped forward.

"Is this one that clips in the front?" he asked, slipping a finger under the elastic of the shoulder strap of her bra.

"Jake Redhorse," she said, her voice now a sweet combination of mock shock and humor. "How do you know about that?"

He grinned. "I've seen a few things since we were kids."

Her grin widened, and she reached for the clasp. "Well, I should hope so."

Lori opened the bra between her breasts and slipped it off like a shoulder holster. Her breasts were heavy and round and he wanted to kiss her. But he waited. Something about that smile kept him pinned to the spot as she placed her hands on her hips and slipped the scrap of fabric down. The lace rolled up like a leaf of tobacco as she stepped clear. And there she was, naked and his at last.

"Lori. You're so beautiful."

Her smile held a promise he intended for her to keep.

"And you are still dressed."

He wasn't, really. Only a T-shirt and his trousers separated them. But not for long. He ignored the twinge of pain as he leaned back against the counter to pull off his shoes and socks. Her warm fingers danced over his hips as she lifted the cotton shirt. He raised his arms, and she drew the garment swiftly away.

Jake bit his lip at the hitch of pain the movement caused as he lowered his arms, resisting the impulse to lift a hand up to cover his injury. When he straightened, it was to find Lori clutching his top in one fist. Her lush, inviting smile faltered and her brow knit.

"Oh, Jake. Look at you." She stepped forward to gently run her fingers over the purple bruises that marked his torso.

"I'm all right, Lori." He wasn't going to let a few bruises stop him from showing Lori exactly what he could give her. He could provide for her and protect her. He could be a father to Fortune and a husband to Lori. If she'd just say yes.

But first he wanted to remind her of how good they were together.

Her fingers continued to dance over the marks left by their attacker. Bullets stopped by his vest, but the impact had damaged his skin and muscle. The bruises had spread, the marks reminiscent of the injuries she had seen as the result of auto accidents.

"I don't know how this didn't break a rib," she said.

He took hold of her wrists, stopping her. "It didn't. And I took an aspirin before dinner."

"Aspirin makes you bleed more!"

"Ibuprofen, then. Lori, I don't need a nurse right now."

She straightened. "What do you need?"

"I need you, Lori."

She blinked up at him, indecision plain on her face. "Are you sure?"

"Letting go will hurt me more."

Her kiss was gentle, and his response left no doubt that he wanted her passion, not her tenderness. Her hands slipped down his taut stomach and brushed over his aroused flesh.

"What about protection?" she asked.

He met her gaze. "You're using something. Want a backup?"

She lifted her brows and gave him a contemplative gaze. Was she surprised he was leaving it up to her? She'd always been the more responsible one.

"I trust you, Lori. I'm sorry if I ever made you feel otherwise."

She threw her arms about him, molding their bodies together. Then they were kissing again, hungry mouths full of promise and want. He retrieved a condom, opening the single packet. Lori took it from him, her fingers stroking and teasing as she slipped it over him. With a rush of need and desire, he took her in the shower. Afterward, he washed her body before allowing her to do the same for him. The results of her touch roused him again, and he left the shower with Lori in his arms, taking her to the bed. When at last they settled to sleep, he was certain that she knew what was in his heart, because he had told her everything with his loving. He trusted her with all he was, and he loved her with his whole heart.

They slept soundly, entwined in each other's arms. Sometime later he felt her rise, heard the soft cries of a baby and then felt her return to his side.

Jake woke to the buzz of his cell phone vibrating on the nightstand. Lori's arm was across his bare chest. He reached for the phone and she rolled away. He checked the display. It was his brother Ty—calling him at five o'clock in the morning.

Jake slid from the bed as he answered, then collected his scattered clothing as he exited the room where Lori slept.

Lori weaved toward Fortune, half-asleep and eyes squinting against the light now coming through the window. Night, she realized, was turning to day. The changing table was in the other bedroom. Lori carried Fortune across the hall, changed Fortune's wet diaper and headed with her to the kitchen to make formula, where she discovered a different agent sitting at the dining room table scrolling through emails on a laptop.

"Good morning, Ms. Mott," he said. "There's coffee on."

She gave an appropriate reply but found her throat had a frog in it. Did all the agents have such precise haircuts?

After Fortune was happily draining a bottle and quiet except for the sound of her greedy sucking, she turned to the new man.

"I'm Lori."

"Yes, ma'am. Agent Ronald Clifford."

She smiled and nodded. "Any news?"

"Yes, ma'am. Officer Redhorse apprehended a suspect, Faras Pike, wanted in connection with this case."

"Officer Redhorse?" Lori frowned in confusion and glanced toward the room where she thought Jake had still been sleeping.

She looked back to Clifford. "Isn't he here?"

Chapter Twenty

"No, ma'am," said FBI field agent Clifford in response to Lori's question about Jake. "Officer Redhorse is back on the job."

"What?"

"Reassigned, ma'am, by his supervisor."

Reassigned, from his protection detail? Of course—with manpower so short on the rez, Chief Tinnin would not need Jake to protect her or the baby. That was now the job of the FBI. But for how long?

Was it over between them again? Just like that?

She could not believe that Jake would leave Fortune. It didn't seem possible when he'd been so adamant about taking custody.

"I see." She resisted the urge to retrieve her phone from the charger and call Jake.

"What will happen now?" she asked.

"Ma'am?"

"I mean with the baby."

"Temporary placement in an undisclosed location. She'll be safe, Ms. Mott."

The ache began in Lori's chest and moved out to

cramp her stomach and squeeze her lungs. They were going to take Fortune away from her. She was going to lose another baby and Jake all over again.

"Excuse me," she said, then ducked her head and hustled down the hallway to the room where she should have spent the night. Jake had been right to want to keep Fortune on tribal lands. Now the FBI had her and Fortune. How would she get them back home?

Once inside, Lori sat like a stone, feeding Fortune as the tears rolled down her face. Only after Fortune was happily gurgling in her bassinet did Lori indulge in clinging to a pillow and weeping. This was why she had not gone back to Jake. She'd known deep down that he'd never loved her, and even if he did, it wasn't enough to stay and protect her from the FBI. But she admitted to herself that she loved him with all her torn and battered heart.

Sometime later she rose, showered and dressed. She was braiding her damp hair when there was a tapping at her door. She swiped at her eyes.

"Yes?"

The door swung open, and there stood Jake Redhorse in a dusty uniform with his hat in his hand. His smile dropped when he looked at her. The shower, it seemed, had not obliterated all signs of her tears. She remained where she was, resisting the urge to run to him.

"Lori?"

"You're back," she whispered.

"Of course I'm back." He cocked his head, his expression puzzled.

"The agent said you were reassigned."

His dark brows lifted in understanding. "Oh. Yes, I did tell him that."

A lie? She wasn't sure, but her heartbeat increased as a stupid, unreasonable hope lifted within her.

He inched into the room and glanced at Fortune, who squealed at the sight of him and beat her arms up and down. He grinned and scooped her up, giving her a greeting in Tonto Apache and then bouncing her against his chest. He carried Fortune across the room and knelt before Lori.

"Why are you crying, Lori?" he asked.

"I'm not. I *was* crying." The lie was obvious. "So where were you, then?"

"I met with Faras," he said.

Her sorrow now turned to anxiety as her gaze swept him for injuries.

"You're all right?"

He nodded.

"I don't understand. Why would you go to him?"

He returned Fortune to the crib and came to sit beside her on the bed.

She sat beside him, her legs hanging limp over the edge of the mattress. She felt like a damp, discarded bath towel. It seemed a great effort to move.

"Wait, did you say you arrested Faras or met with him?"

"We had a little chat. He wasn't arrested. Ty set up a meeting for me."

She did not like the sound of that. Now she wasn't sad so much as frightened. What had he done?

"I told Faras that the baby has been blood typed, prints and DNA taken."

"Which is why they wanted her dead."

"He never admitted involvement, but yes, I think so, too. He knows the feds have custody of her now."

Lori was about to tell Jake that she had custody and she wasn't giving Fortune up to the FBI. But she didn't say that because it occurred to her that the FBI might be the only ones who could protect this baby she now thought of as her own.

But Fortune wasn't hers. Never had been, really. She'd been called in as a nurse to do a job. She'd done it, and now it was time to let go.

She sniffed. Why had she let herself fall in love with Fortune? After all this time. All the babies she had cared for, and she'd never felt like this.

"Faras denies any culpability in the actions of either Earle Glass or Minnie Cobb. He suggested that the pair wanted to sell the baby on the black market."

"Do you believe him?"

"It's possible."

"That wasn't what I asked."

"No. I don't believe him. He knows exactly what his people are doing because he sent them to get Fortune. The important thing is that he has told me that none of his people will try again to retrieve the baby."

"What does that mean?"

"He doesn't want her."

"Why did they want her to begin with?"

"He didn't say."

Lori glanced at Fortune, who was unaware, of course, of her peril. "Do you believe him?"

"Yes, but…"

"What?" she asked.

"Ty beat me to it."

"To what?"

"Making a deal. I'm afraid Ty is the one who convinced him to protect Fortune, which means Ty owes Faras a favor. A big favor."

The kind of favor that could land Ty in prison, Lori thought. Now her mood matched Jake's as the worry tugged at her.

"What about your brother Ty? Bear Den guessed that he was at Gill's place the morning of the shooting, right?"

"Yes. Bear Den spoke to Ty, who admitted to being at Gill's place but claims he was guarding us, which I believe."

"Does Bear Den believe it?"

"Doesn't matter. Bear Den can't prove a connection to Earle or Minnie, so Ty is in the clear for now."

"Is Fortune safe?"

"Yes, because of whatever deal Ty made and because Faras knows that my entire force will hold him responsible if anything happens to that baby."

"He has more men than our police force," she noted.

"We're getting two more."

"What about Earle Glass? That's Faras's man."

"Faras was willing to let Earle take the blame for

everything. He knows we don't believe that but also knows we can't prove otherwise unless Earle talks, and he won't because Faras will kill him."

"Can't the FBI protect him?"

"Do you want Earle Glass protected?"

Lori said nothing. It was the kind of decision she was happy she did not have to make.

"What about Minnie Cobb? She was after Zella, and I believe she was the one who came after Fortune." Lori just couldn't prove it and had failed to identify her.

"She'll be called off."

Lori nodded. She understood the deal but was still uncomfortable with it.

"Faras again?" she asked.

"Minnie belongs to the Wolf Posse. So she answers to Faras."

"Does Tinnin know you spoke to Faras?"

Jake shook his head. "No way."

"You could have been killed doing that." She wanted to clutch his arm. But she remained seated with one leg splayed out on the mattress so that she now faced him.

"Killed?" He scoffed. "I could get fired."

That confident grin made her chest squeeze, and another tear rolled down her damp cheek.

"I thought this would make you happy. She's safe."

But not ours any longer.

Lori nodded. "But there's still something going on with the missing girls."

Jake's face went hard and his brow dropped. "The

force is investigating, and we're collaborating our efforts with the FBI Sex Crimes unit. We'll find them, and we will bring them home."

Lori was certain Jake would never give up. She hoped the girls were still alive, but she worried that the attention and the investigation might spook whoever held them. Surely Faras Pike knew who that was.

"Any hits on the DNA?" asked Lori.

"None. Sample and report remain on file," Jake said.

"There's something else," he continued. "We have spoken to Zella and her mother about the baby."

Lori braced herself. She remembered what it had been like telling her own mother that she was pregnant. The shame and the guilt still scorched.

"Yes?" She pressed a hand over her thudding heart, as if that might make the ache less painful.

Jake made a face at the memory.

"How did her mother take it?"

"I don't think she cares one way or the other. She signed the adoption paperwork as Zella's guardian to relinquish custody of the baby. She knows Zella is going to live on the Black Mountain rez, but if she is happy or upset, I couldn't tell. I think she's on something. Maybe just drinking too much. Hard to say."

"So sad."

Lori bowed her head. Zella was only fifteen. She had a crappy home life, which was probably why the gang had targeted her to begin with.

"She'll be better off on Black Mountain," said Jake. "She's been living out in her shelter as much as in her mother's house, and I don't think her mother even noticed."

"Poor kid," whispered Lori.

Lori knew that the last thing Mrs. Colelay needed was another child. Lori thought she had at least seven, and one was still in diapers. She had seen him at the clinic for booster shots. But Mrs. Colelay could still demand custody of her daughter's child.

"The tribe has accepted the Colelays' paperwork relinquishing parental rights and agreed to allow the child Zella delivered to be placed up for adoption within the tribe."

That was good. Wasn't it?

Lori's gaze drifted to the baby, kicking her feet in the legless sack she now wore.

So Zella was safe and would have a better home. Fortune was safe from whoever had been chasing her, and Ty's involvement in this matter was to remain secret. And just like that, the threat dissolved, taking with it some of the starch from her spine. Lori could go back to her life. Her cold, sterile, safe life.

Only, she couldn't. She wasn't that woman any longer. She'd opened her heart again. Against her better judgment, she'd let Jake and the baby crawl inside. What in the wide world was she going to do now?

"It's over," she whispered. "Isn't it?"

Jake smiled and nodded. But she didn't smile back.

Chapter Twenty-One

Lori sat in the temporary tribal seat in Koun'nde, waiting for the closed session of the tribal council. Fortune slept, cradled in her arms. Beside Lori sat Jake, leaning forward with his elbows on his knees, spinning his hat in circles by the brim as he waited for the council to fill the seven empty chairs set around the large circular table inlaid with the turquoise for which their tribe was named. To her right sat Kenshaw Little Falcon, the tribe's shaman. The council remained out on the porch conducting a preliminary meeting.

"Heck with this," Jake said at last and rose to go to them.

Kenshaw watched him, then turned to Lori. "You can't rush them. I've tried."

Kenshaw Little Falcon had the lined face of a senior citizen, but his hair retained some of its once-dark color so that it grew in streaks of black and white. He'd dressed up for the occasion, which meant he wore a clean denim shirt and one of his best turquoise necklaces. This one was strung with turquoise beads that grew in size until they met the large silver medallion of a thunderbird. Lori knew Little Falcon was more than the tribe's spiritual leader. He was also the head of the tribe's medicine society, the Turquoise Guardians, of which she and Jake were the newest members. In addition, he headed the elite warrior subsect, Tribal Thunder. Kenshaw had also presided over her daughter's funeral five years earlier.

"So you and Jake will both agree to shared custody?" he asked. She nodded. "What does your mother think of that?"

Lori thought back to the conversation, and the ache returned to her heart.

"She said it was about time I snagged a man."

Kenshaw nodded. "Unfortunate. She should be proud of you. It's an honorable thing you do, to care for a child who is orphaned."

Her mother did not care much for honor. Mostly she cared for herself and her bottle. All else took a back seat.

Kenshaw was looking through the window at the men and women on the porch. "It is possible that they will choose just one of you, because you are not married." Kenshaw was ordained as a minister by the state. He had once agreed to perform their marriage ceremony.

"We'll see," said Lori, but the panic was back.

"Are you willing to take custody from Jake to have her?" he asked.

"No, of course not."

"What if they say that a child should be raised by a woman?"

"That's sexist."

"Still, there is a reason that women bear children and men protect and provide. I know that the council leans toward one guardian. My feeling is that it will be you, Lori."

She swallowed her dread at this. She couldn't let them take the infant from Jake. It would kill him.

"Hard to lose two baby girls," said Kenshaw.

"Yes."

Kenshaw cocked his head but remained sitting forward, giving her his profile as he spoke.

"Have you two considered marriage?" he asked.

"He hasn't asked me," she said.

He shifted, finally looking at her, showing his dark, perceptive eyes. "Maybe you ask him this time."

"Is that what the tribe wants?" She forced a smile. It would make their decision easier, of course, if she and Jake were engaged.

He smiled. "No, Lori. It's what you want."

"He doesn't love me, Kenshaw."

"Are you sure?"

"He's never said so."

Kenshaw sat back. "Some men say so in words, others in actions. I think he has been telling you that he loves you for a long time now, if you would only listen with your heart instead of your ears."

Was it true? She looked at Jake through the windows, now standing with the council on the porch.

Kenshaw lifted his medallion and then let it thump

back to his chest. "Of course, even if you ask him, maybe you can come see me a few times to talk."

"About what?"

"Whatever has kept you stuck like a vein of turquoise in rock for five years."

Now Lori half turned to face him. "I'd like that."

Kenshaw reached out a thick, gnarled finger and offered it to Fortune, who clasped hold. Lori smiled down at the girl, who was yawning and blinking wearily. She released Kenshaw.

"Nothing like a baby to make you stay in the moment," he said.

That was very true.

"My wife is also a good listener. Psychologist, you know."

Lori nodded. "Yes, I'd considered seeing her once. I actually canceled three appointments." He smiled. Perhaps he already knew that she had done that. But now she felt ready to go back and then forward. "I won't cancel the next one."

Kenshaw smiled and turned toward the sound behind them. The council was arriving, filing in and taking their seats. Jake came back to his place, and she stood to meet him.

"Can I speak to you?" she said.

He glanced toward the council. "Now?"

"Do you trust me?"

Jake smiled. "Yes, I do."

She tugged him toward the door. He used his palm to set his hat on his head and followed her out to the porch. The night was cool, and she tucked Fortune inside her coat as she stopped to speak to Jake.

"Kenshaw says they are leaning toward one guardian."

It was as if she had thrown a bucket of ice water in his face.

"Did he?" asked Jake. His heart was hammering now, and he was sweating despite the chill in the air. Was Lori going to fight him over custody?

"He also said I should go speak to his wife about, you know, my feelings of loss."

"That's a good idea. For both of us." He glanced back through the picture window. The council members were all settling into their seats and he wanted to get back in there, but he sensed Lori wasn't finished. "What else did he say?"

"He also suggested that I ask you to marry me."

His smile dropped away, and his gaze flashed to hers. Was she asking? His heart seemed to stop as he tried to read her expression.

"Because of the custody for Fortune?" he asked.

He hated the thought that they were right back where they'd started and that Lori was trapped once more, having to marry him instead of wanting to marry him. Did she understand that he loved her?

He had a crashing realization. He'd been so busy seeing Faras and speaking with Ty, Bear Den, Tinnin and then with Kenshaw that he had not had a chance to speak to Lori, to tell her that he loved her.

Why did the universe keep doing this to them?

"Lori, I don't want you to have to marry me to have Fortune."

"There are lots of good reasons to marry you, Jake. Fortune is an important one, and it would make the council's decision simple. It would almost guarantee you custody of this baby. It would make it easier for us to care for her, and it would give her a home with two parents who both already love her."

All of that was true. So why was his heart now aching with each damn beat?

"Yes," he whispered, feeling the leaden certainty sinking farther down in his stomach.

"But that's not why I'm asking you to marry me."

He peered at her from under his eyebrows as a trickle of hope slipped over the ache.

"I'm asking you, Jake Redhorse, because I love you. And I'd like to try again, as grown-ups this time." She took hold of one hand and squeezed his cold fingers. "So, Officer Redhorse, will you be my husband?"

He reached with his free hand, took hold of the back of her neck and pulled her toward him.

"Yes," he said against her lips and then kissed her with all the hope and joy that now pulsed through his heart.

They would be a family together, and with the grace of the universe shining down upon them, there would be more children to follow. Jake wrapped his arms around Lori and Fortune, knowing that he was finally in the right place at the right time—and, most important, with the ones he loved.

Epilogue

Lori opted for a traditional wedding dress of white, with white lilies pinned in her dark hair. She carried no bouquet but instead baby Fortune, also dressed in white, the long hem of her baptism gown trailing over Lori's arm. As a Catholic, she wished to be wed in a church while including one of the traditional blessings of her people.

The music was supplied by Jake's brother Ty, who was a talented flute player. The quavering sweet notes of the bridal march signaled her time to begin. The guests all rose as her sisters, Amelia, Jocelyn, Rosa and Dominique, preceded her down the aisle. She clasped her mother's arm with her free one and set them in motion, walking down the aisle of the Catholic church in Koun'nde. Her mother wore a lily pinned to her yellow dress and seemed sober, though Lori recognized that vacant smile and unsteady tread well enough to know otherwise. She understood now that many of Jake's mother's concerns came from Lori's mother and Lori's upbringing. And Jake's apprehensions came from not wanting to disappoint his mother.

She could not see Jake yet but knew he was there, waiting for her. Maybe it was all necessary, the time and the pain, to help her appreciate what she now had: a career that gave her life meaning, the beginning of a family to love and support, and a good man whom she had loved since he was a boy. And he loved her, had always loved her.

She passed her friends from high school, from college and from her job. Nina cast her a little wave, Verna gave her a thumbs-up and Burl cried. She saw Jake's coworkers now, Jack Bear Den standing a full head taller than anyone near him, and Chief Tinnin beside Carol Dorset, who wept a steady stream of tears.

Jake's mother came into view, in a pink dress that fell to the floor and covered the healing sore on her ankle. She met Lori's gaze, and though she did not offer a smile, she did incline her head in a nod of approval. Lori acknowledged that neither she nor any mortal woman would ever be good enough for May's favorite son. But May accepted this marriage, and Lori took her at her word. She would not come between them again. And Lori knew why.

Beside May was her new husband, Duffy Rope, whom Lori was just beginning to know. Duffy had made a point of telling Lori all about a certain conversation that Jake had had with his mother when he had told her that their early pregnancy was his fault for not using protection, and that if she didn't lay off this topic and treat Lori with respect, he would stop coming around.

Lori offered Duffy a bright smile as she passed, which he returned.

On the opposite side of the aisle stood Lori's mother's newest live-in boyfriend, whose eyes seemed glassy. Her mother waved to him as Lori's sisters continued steadily on before them down the aisle, where the priest and their shaman both waited to perform the ceremony. Unfortunately, they blocked her view of the priest, the shaman and Jake.

Her smile brightened as she anticipated the blessing that Kenshaw would speak and that Lori knew by heart because she had heard it at her older sisters' weddings. Their shaman would ceremonially tie their wrists together to symbolize that from this day forward she and Jake would be two people with one life. It was a tradition of her people but also of her father's people called handfasting,

In Tonto Apache, the shaman would tell all gathered here that from this day forward this couple would feel no rain or cold or loneliness for each would bestow the other with shelter, warmth and comfort. Then Kenshaw would bless them and ask that their days together be good and their time on this earth be long before turning the sermon over to the priest.

Lori reached the end of the rows of guests and finally saw Jake's groomsmen. Both Ty and Kee faced her, standing side by side. Ty held the flute to his lips, continuing to play as she neared her place. Unfortunately, Jake's youngest brother, Colt, could not be coaxed down from his isolation to see his brother wed. So Jake had chosen two of the men from the tribal police force, Daniel Wetselline and Harold Shea, selected to balance her four sisters and bridesmaids. Her sisters looked so beautiful in their full-length red dresses as they filed into their places opposite the men. Kee stood still as a statue beside Officer Wetselline, grinning broadly at her. In sharp contrast, to Kee's right, Ty swayed as he played his flute, looking out of character but very handsome in his dark suit and multiple strands of long, beaded turquoise necklaces. And finally Dominique stepped aside, allowing her a view of her handsome groom.

The smile Jake gave her bathed her in joy and hope. She stood a moment to gaze at him, trying to fix the memory in her mind for always. He stood waiting, but she would make him wait no longer. He had given her his trust and defended her from both their enemies and his family. Now she looked forward to today and tomorrow and all the tomorrows that came after that.

Today they married, not for the baby or their tribe or to please their parents, but because when you loved a man as she loved Jake, that was simply the only course.

Together, she and Jake and baby Fortune would become the family they were always meant to be.

* * * * *

COMING NEXT MONTH FROM
◆ HARLEQUIN®

INTRIGUE

Available March 20, 2018

#1773 ROUGHSHOD JUSTICE
Blue River Ranch • by Delores Fossen
It's been two years since Texas Ranger Jameson Beckett has seen Kelly Stockwell. Now she's crashed back into his life with a toddler and no memory of their once-intense relationship.

#1774 SUDDEN SETUP
Crisis: Cattle Barge • by Barb Han
Ella Butler wasn't expecting rescue in the form of Holden Crawford, a perfect stranger. But will his protection be enough to save her from ruthless killers, let alone absolve him of his own dark past?

#1775 DROPPING THE HAMMER
The Kavanaughs • by Joanna Wayne
After a brutal kidnapping, Rachel Maxwell isn't sure she's still the powerful attorney she once was. Cowboy Luke Dawkins is also trying to escape a troubled past, and maybe they can remind each other what true strength— and love—looks like.

#1776 DESPERATE STRANGERS
by Carla Cassidy
Julie Peterson's amnesia gives Nick Simon the perfect alibi—after all, she doesn't realize that she only just met her "fiancé" at the scene of a crime. But can she trust Nick as her only protector when a dangerous killer draws close?

#1777 TRIBAL BLOOD
Apache Protectors: Wolf Den • by Jenna Kernan
His time with the marines left him speechless with nightmares, but when pregnant Kasey Doka escapes a surrogacy ring and seeks out his help, Colt Redhorse feels something between them that goes deeper than words.

#1778 FEDERAL AGENT UNDER FIRE
Protectors of Cade County • by Julie Anne Lindsey
For years FBI agent Blake Garrett has obsessed over a serial killer...a killer who has now become obsessed with the one woman to escape with her life—Melissa Lane. Can Blake protect her without his fixation clouding his judgment?

YOU CAN FIND MORE INFORMATION ON UPCOMING HARLEQUIN® TITLES, FREE EXCERPTS AND MORE AT WWW.HARLEQUIN.COM.

HICNM0318

Get 2 Free Books,

Plus 2 Free Gifts—

just for trying the Reader Service!

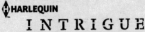

HI17R2

SPECIAL EXCERPT FROM

▶ mira

A killer stole her voice. Now she's ready to take it back.
Don't miss the next chilling installment in the
SHADES OF DEATH *series*
from USA TODAY *bestselling author Debra Webb.*

Turn the page for a sneak peek from
THE LONGEST SILENCE
by **Debra Webb**, *coming March 2018.*

New York Times *bestselling author Sandra Brown*
calls it "a gripping read."

The phone wouldn't stop ringing. The annoying sound echoed off the dingy walls of the tiny one-room apartment.

Joanna Guthrie chewed her thumbnail as she stared at the damned cell phone. Three people had this number: her boss, a research analyst she occasionally worked with and Ellen. If it was work, the caller would simply leave a message, but it wasn't work—it was Ellen.

Jo's foot started to tap so she stood and paced the floor. "Not answering."

Why should she answer? The calls came about three or four times a year and they were always the same. Ellen would complain about her life and her husband and her kids. She would bemoan the hand fate had dealt her. She would never be whole. Nothing she attempted fixed her. Not the shrinks or the meditation or the yoga or any of the other crazier shit she'd tried, like cocaine, and certainly not the alcohol.

The ringing stopped.

Jo stared at the phone. Two minutes tops and it would start that fucking ringing again. She closed her eyes and exhaled a measure of the frustration always generated by calls from Ellen. Guilt immediately took its place. No matter the reason, whenever Ellen called Jo always wound up feeling guilty whether she answered the damned phone or not. A voice mail carried the same guilt-generating effect.

"Not my fault." She paced the room like a freshly incarcerated criminal on the front end of a life sentence.

Ellen had chosen her own path. She'd made the decision to pretend to be normal. Dared to marry and to have children. Jo shook her head. How the hell could she do that after what they'd gone through—what they'd done? Now the woman spent every minute of every day terrified that she would somehow disappoint her family or that something bad would happen to them because of her. Or, worse, that someone would discover her secret—their secret.

MDWEXP1017

Deep breath. "Not my problem."

Jo had made the smarter choice. She'd cut ties with her family and friends. No boyfriends, much less husbands. No kids for damned sure. If she wanted sexual release she either took care of it herself or she picked up a soldier from one of the clubs in Killeen. She didn't go to church; she didn't live in the same town for more than a year. She never shared her history with anyone. Not that there was anything in her past that would give anyone reason to suspect the truth, but she hated the looks of sympathy, the questions.

The past was over and done. Dragging it into the present would not change what was done.

She had boundaries. Boundaries to protect herself. She never wasted time making small talk, much less friends. Besides, she wasn't in one place long enough for anyone to notice or to care. Since her employer was an online newspaper, she rarely had to interact face-to-face with anyone. In fact, she and the boss had never met in person and he was the closest thing to a friend she had.

Whatever that made her, Jo didn't care.

Hysterical laughter bubbled into her throat. Even the IRS didn't have her address. She used the newspaper's address for anything permanent. Her boss faxed her whatever official-looking mail he received, and then shredded it. He never asked why. Jo supposed he understood somehow.

She recognized her behavior for what it was—paranoia. Plain and simple. Six years back she'd noticed one of those health fairs in the town where she'd lived. Probably not the most scientific or advanced technology since it was held in a school cafeteria. Still, she'd been desperate to ensure nothing had been implanted in her body—like some sort of tracking device—so she'd scraped up enough money to pay for a full-body scan. Actually, she'd been short fifty bucks but the tech had accepted a quick fuck in exchange. After all that trouble he'd found nothing. Ultimately that was a good thing but it had pissed her off at the time.

A ring vibrated the air in the room.

Enough. Jo snatched up the phone. "What do you want, Ellen?"

The silence on the other end sent a surge of oily black uncertainty snaking around her heart. When she would have ended the call, words tumbled across the dead air.

"This is Ellen's husband."

A new level of doubt nudged at Jo. "Art?"

She had no idea how she'd remembered the man's name. Personal details were something else she had obliterated from her life. Distance and anonymity were her only real friends now.

Now? She almost laughed out loud at her vast understatement. Eighteen years. She'd left any semblance of a normal life behind eighteen years ago. Jesus Christ, had it only been eighteen?

Don't miss
THE LONGEST SILENCE,
available March 2018 wherever
MIRA® Books and ebooks are sold.

www.Harlequin.com